Stories by Contemporary Writers from Shanghai

THE 17-YEAR-OLD HUSSARS

T0192962

This book is edited and designed by the Editorial Committee of *Cultural China* series

Text by Lu Nei
Translation by:
 Zhu Jingwen (*The Tale of Forty Crows' Furious Battle*, *Carrying a Girl on the Back to Mozhen Township*, *Christmas Eve of 1991*, *You Are a Witch*, *Knifed Buttocks*, *The First Generation ID Card*, *No One Was Innocent*)
 Anna Holmwood (*Monsters at Volleyball*)
 Chris Burrow (*The Book Thief*)
 Rachel Henson (*Keep Running, Little Brother*)
Cover Image by Quanjing
Interior Design by Xue Wenqing
Cover Design by Wang Wei

Editor: Cao Yue
Editorial Director: Zhang Yicong

Senior Consultants: Sun Yong, Wu Ying, Yang Xinci
Managing Director and Publisher: Wang Youbu

ISBN: 978-1-60220-258-0

Address any comments about *The 17-Year-Old Hussars* to:

Better Link Press
99 Park Ave
New York, NY 10016
USA

or

Shanghai Press and Publishing Development Company, Ltd.
F 7 Donghu Road, Shanghai, China (200031)
Email: comments_betterlinkpress@hotmail.com

Printed in China by Shenzhen Donnelley Printing Co., Ltd.
1   3   5   7   9   10   8   6   4   2

THE 17-YEAR-OLD HUSSARS

By Lu Nei

Better Link Press

Foreword

This collection of books for English readers consists of short stories and novellas published by writers based in Shanghai. Apart from a few who are immigrants to Shanghai, most of them were born in the city, from the latter part of the 1940s to the 1980s. Some of them had their works published in the late 1970s and the early 1980s; some gained recognition only in the 21st century. The older among them were the focus of the "To the Mountains and Villages" campaign in their youth, and as a result, lived and worked in the villages. The difficult paths of their lives had given them unique experiences and perspectives prior to their eventual return to Shanghai. They took up creative writing for different reasons but all share a creative urge and a love for writing. By profession, some of them are college professors, some literary editors, some directors of literary institutions, some freelance writers and some professional writers. From the individual styles of the authors and the art of their writings, readers can easily detect traces of the authors' own experiences in life, their interests, as well as their aesthetic values. Most of the works in this collection are still written in the realistic style that represents, in a painstakingly fashioned fictional world, the changes of the times in urban and rural life. Having grown up in a more open era, the younger writers have been spared the hardships experienced by their predecessors, and therefore seek greater freedom in their writing. Whatever category of writers they belong to, all of them have gained their rightful places in Chinese literary circles over the last forty years. Shanghai writers tend to favor urban narratives more than other genres of writing. Most of the works in this collection can be characterized as urban literature with Shanghai characteristics, but there are also exceptions.

Called the "Paris of the East," Shanghai was already an international metropolis in the 1920s and 30s. Being the center of China's economy, culture and literature at the time, it housed a majority of writers of importance in the history of modern Chinese literature. The list includes Lu Xun, Guo Moruo, Mao Dun and Ba Jin, who had all written and published prolifically in Shanghai. Now, with Shanghai re-emerging as a globalized metropolis, the Shanghai writers who have appeared on the literary scene in the last forty years all face new challenges and literary quests of the times. I am confident that some of the older writers will produce new masterpieces. As for the fledging new generation of writers, we naturally expect them to go far in their long writing careers ahead of them. In due course, we will also introduce those writers who did not make it into this collection.

Wang Jiren
Series Editor

Contents

The 17-Year-Old Hussars

The Tale of Forty Crows' Furious Battle

All of us, without exception, were damn near frozen to death in the winter of 1991. Almost all of us were reduced to skin and bones, except Hog's Intestine; we suspect his obesity was caused by a pituitary gland disorder. But even he was damn near frozen to death.

Ours was a machinery maintenance class of forty boys and no girls. All the girls in the world seemed to have died that year. After spending two years at this technical school, we had all become sexually frustrated youths—we were on the verge of breaking down, and eked out our lives from one minute to the next. It was an extremely cold winter, cold to the point that your brain would cease to function, even when it came to girls.

Forty boys were supposed to bicycle to an assembly plant in the suburbs for on-the-job training. On our way to the faraway plant, a succession of tall buildings, low buildings, the city wall, the canal, the fields, paved road and finally the pagoda would come into our view. The pagoda was on a remote mountain; on the other side of the mountain was a quarry where the prisoners were kept. Big Ass's older brother worked there, and Yellow Hair's uncle was a warden. Once we arrived at the plant, we all dismounted and hurriedly left our bikes in the bike shed. Coming out of the shed, you could see the pagoda that was still so far away.

On the first day of training, we had wreaked havoc on the cafeteria's steam room where the workers' lunch boxes were being heated on the racks of a refrigerator-like device. I had no idea what it was called and I never even bothered to find out. At lunch break, workers were supposed to go there and fetch their own lunch boxes. That very first day we didn't bring our own lunches, and since what was offered in the cafeteria was way too expensive, forty of us all went to fetch something from the racks. In a short span of ten minutes, as the workers were still sauntering toward the cafeteria, all the lunch boxes and enamel teacups had been cleaned out of all contents.

After that meal, the general manager of the assembly plant was almost on his knees when he pled with our teacher. "We cannot afford to have these forty bastards around; you might as well leave for good."

Exasperated, it was our teacher's turn to almost get down on his knees towards the general manager. "Could you kindly agree to have them as apprentices here for just two months, and I promise you there will be no more meal-snatching and no more misbehavior."

He then immediately censured Big Ass, who had led the charge to the lunch boxes. With that reprimand on his record, Big Ass would have to settle for a job at the fertilizer plant for life.

I had shared the lunch in a pink enamel teacup with Iron Monk. It was stewed pork hock with winter bamboo shoots, a much better choice than the others. It was pure luck, since none of the others had tried to uncover what was in the pink enamel teacup, for reasons unknown. We fled the scene soon after we finished eating the food inside. But I seemed to remember that the pink enamel teacup had a string of grape design on it and looked pleasant enough.

Before the approach of winter, the workshop manager ordered us to wipe all the windows clean and knock out all the cracked ones so that he could ask for replacements. Most of the windows at the workshop were cracked; they might not look good aesthetically, but they were nice windbreaks. After a round of whimsical smashing by more than forty boys with hammers, all the glass was broken and the wind started blowing in. Feeling cold, the manager ran to the General Affairs Office for the replacement of fifty pieces of glass, only to see his request being thrown out.

As a result, we spent that whole winter in the workshop without even one windowpane left standing. Frustrated, the workers had to cover the holes with newspapers. The night before the cold front descended from the north, we were hit with a storm; all the newspapers became mushy and tattered. No one was willing to put up the newspaper again, even it meant we all had to brave the cold.

We accepted the bad days by choice, and the good days by pure luck.

Forty boys were in charge of a wheelbarrow that was supposed to transport at least ten cubic meters of mud out of the plant. We had no tools, no spades, not even a dustpan. Forty pairs of eyes, plus a few eyeglasses here and there, all stared at this pile of sludge. At first, we managed to use our hands to pick up a few clumps and throw them in the wheelbarrow, but as the pile felt more and more like the fresh cow dung, we soon stopped working. Squatting by the pile, we started smoking, prancing around and doing push-ups. I was pushing the wheelbarrow full of the little clumps we gathered toward the plant entrance when I saw a forklift coming my way. Unable to maneuver the wheelbarrow away, I made a dash to the side without it, and as the forklift crashed head-on into the barrow, there was a huge noise. Two of its wheels came off and were coming our way like two huge barbells. The metal hopper was also blown away somewhere. The female operator of the forklift was so frightened, her face turned livid red, and she jumped down from the cab, curses pouring out of her mouth.

With the wheelbarrow gone, we smoked. As the end of the workday approached, the workshop manager came with a spade on his shoulder; he wanted us to work overtime to get the sludge out. But upon seeing the wheelbarrow in its present state, he was left dumbfounded. We wheezed by him triumphantly on our bicycles.

The very day the cold front arrived, everything seemed to have shriveled in seconds, including our facial skin. The forty of us were still in shirtsleeves. In fact, whatever you wore didn't really make that much difference, since no cotton jacket could stop the cold air if you had to get around on a bicycle in the winter of 1991.

The minute Hog's Intestine jumped on his bicycle, the two valve cores popped out like bullets. Hog's Intestine weighed about one hundred and forty kilos and was abnormally fat; even the tires of the good Phoenix brand bicycle couldn't stand being jumped on and off by someone of his girth. After we left, he had to push his bicycle into town on foot for repair. It just so happened that none of the repair guys were around. Hog's Intestine got pneumonia. He was no longer required to work as an intern. Now we were left with forty minus one. For the sake of convenience, we still thought ourselves as a group of forty. Even if Hog's Intestine died, we would still save a bowl and a pair of chopsticks for him.

The forty of us sat in the dark and dingy workshop. It was snowing outside, and the sky looked as dreary as a sheet of tinplate. Orange-colored lights were on here and there inside the workshop, coming probably from the bulbs of the lathes, drilling machines, shaping machines or milling machines. None of us knew the difference between a lathe and a shaping machine. Under the annoyingly glare of the lights, we passed around cigarettes, the Red Pagoda Mountain brand cigarettes.

All the workers curled up in the lounge where the stove was; a pot of water was boiling on the stove. The place was warm, but the forty of us were barred from there. All we could do was squat near the entrance, lay down the straw sacks we picked up as mats, and sit or stretch out on them. As one could easily freeze to the point of losing consciousness, to keep ourselves alert we moved to strip Egg Seven of his pants. He didn't put up a fight at first, and by the time he was ready to fight it, his pants were already gone. With his buttocks bare, he wrapped himself up with a Hawaiian-style straw skirt made of hay sacks and searched everywhere for his pants. Later, Toe Corn walked behind him and set his straw skirt on fire with a cigarette lighter.

After this round of horseplay, we all felt much warmer.

Among the forty of us, Impotent Yang wore glasses. He was good at drawing, a craft he had learned from his grandfather, who we heard was a sugarcoated figurine artist. He used a carbon stick to draw a life-size nude female on the wall, with areolae as big as coins. Awed by this masterpiece, we all stepped back and squinted at the drawing. Impotent Yang added, "The bigger the picture, the bigger the arousal effect; all the porn pictures you have seen were at most palm-sized, and were hardly artistically shocking."

Squinting Eyes had an erection, poor thing—even a look at a carbon drawing could cause him to become erect.

It snowed for many days. And that was the number of days we, the forty boys in dark gray uniforms, huddled under the storage cover outside the warehouse. But the cover only offered protection against the snow, and not the wind. We decided to send a student representative to negotiate with the factory for a room with walls. In the end, our class monitor, Sister Nine, together with Rod, a Communist Youth League member, placed a call to our head teacher, telling him that we couldn't stand the freezing cold anymore. The head teacher's response was that we should emulate the soldiers who guard the frontiers of our motherland.

At that time, we were already as frozen as crows just rescued from water. First we lost sensation in our ears, and noses were the next to go, followed by our toes, and gradually I seemed to have entrusted my whole body to someone else who then took me through the heavy snow to a cape-like spot. Aside from the still-beating heart, all my organs had called it quits.

After the phone call, Sister Nine and Rod stopped at the factory entrance for a bowl of hot soy milk to warm themselves up and a few cigarettes, before running back to us for the response. They both were stunned by what came into view: the storage cover had collapsed; metal frames were juxtaposed with asphalt and the snow. The scene somehow looked like a chocolate sundae.

This was the work of Fire Can. He had been waiting for news from Sister Nine and Rod for a long time. While we were on the verge of being frozen to sleep he was running in the snow, and as he got high on running, he kicked on one of the iron posts. The creaking and cackling sound that ensued, similar to the noise preceded the cave-in of a mine shaft, awakened us. Being young and agile, we all leapt to safety in no time. Then, with a huge roar, the storage cover collapsed under heavy snow.

We were lucky that it was a chocolate sundae and not a damned strawberry sundae.

The Number One Exterminator, the fiercest and strongest among us forty boys, as well as the one with the best family background, slipped as he ran for safety. His two front teeth were knocked out. It was not considered a serious injury. But the sad thing was, the teeth had been knocked out in a fight before and the ones he lost this time were the replacements. They were more than front teeth—they were money. If they were merely his front teeth, he probably would not have felt half as bad.

Before our shift was over, we went to wash at the staff bath to warm ourselves a little. It was very quiet there, with none of the factory staff present. We stripped ourselves naked and rushed into the bath. There was no water in the big bath, so we had no choice but to take a shower. As the spigot was turned on, the showerhead, after a few heaves and sighs, finally gave out a thin stream of cold water, much like the pee of someone with an enlarged prostate.

Forty butt-naked boys shared four showerheads, ten to a

team, our dicks all shriveled to minute sizes, our goose-bumped skins touching each other. If I had a gun, I could have killed all the workers of this assembly plant.

Forty boys were forty guns, including machine guns, rifles, handguns, shooting spears and red-tasseled spear guns; they might be different in range and firepower, but they served the same purpose.

Now the forty of them were marching in formation toward the old pagoda. It was the same overcast sky, and I couldn't even remember the last time we had seen a glimpse of sunshine. The pagoda seemed close by, but if you wanted to get there on foot it would take forever, as impossible as successfully stripping a girl naked in a dream.

The river came into view. It was frozen, but no one knew for sure if it was frozen solid. And yet the bridge was too far away, so we decided to cross the river on the ice. It was impossible for all forty of us to walk together, and we asked Hairy Monkey to serve as our sentinel. He didn't like the idea, so we grabbed his bicycle key and threw it across the river. Hairy Monkey broke out in a rage, was soon wrestled to the ground and had his sneakers taken off and thrown to the other side. He was forced to leap across the ice with only his socks on. Like a flashy ballet dancer, he dashed lightly across the surface, albeit inelegantly, and got to the other side.

Not a soul was seen on the road. Snow started falling again. We decided to go back.

Hairy Monkey shouted from across the river, no problem, you can all come. He was searching for his key and sneakers as he called out to us. He then cursed aloud, "F--k you, where is my other shoe?"

With his other sneaker in hand, Big Horse shouted back, "It is here, we are heading back now, you can come and fetch it later." He hung the sneaker on a leafless tree limb.

We went past an agricultural school with no walls and saw a

group of boys playing soccer in the snow. Spittoon came up with the idea of snatching a soccer ball from them so that we could have some fun. So we lined up and crouched on the roadside, cigarettes dangling from our lips, prepared to give him our moral support. A second later, Spittoon had a change of heart—he knew that none of us were trustworthy. If a fight broke out, we might all join in the free-for-all, but we might also choose to stay put as outside observers, so he might end up being beaten up or, with him as the ring leader, having someone else beaten up. None of these outcomes appealed to him. And that was how the idea died a premature death.

The pagoda could still be seen from the agricultural school, and I knew that once you climbed to the top of the pagoda, the farther-away quarry would be in sight. Now, crouching on the roadside, we could only look at the pagoda from afar. It seemed farther away from us than before, but its size somehow remained the same. As the snow became heavier, its image only got blurry.

You might fall in love with different girls in different seasons. I had nothing but contempt for women who swore their love for only one type of men. This was definitely not a matter of taste but a sign of problems with their aesthetic values. The law that made me find different girls attractive in different seasons also applied to the other thirty-nine bastards.

For instance, in the faraway summertime you might fall in love with a girl attending a prestigious middle school, the skinny girl with attractive lips who was the daughter of your literature teacher, or a bimbo carrying a watermelon cutter. But in a harsh winter where we were half-frozen, the forty of us boys who were stuck together were more like forty malnourished crows found flying in the works of Van Gogh: we might not be dead in the real sense, but we did have an aura of impending doom around us. In a winter like this, the forty crows could only fall in love with a straw girl.

The straw girl with a folding umbrella went past us in snow, like a flower petal.

Chicken Xiao claimed that she was the girl of his dreams. In a dark grey uniform that was at least two sizes too large, Chicken Xiao was only about five feet tall. Give him a feather duster; he might use it as a mop. I didn't know why he chose to wear such a large-sized uniform. Could it be that he was swayed by the sheer amount of material that came with a larger size? We assumed that the girl of his dreams was just a large-sized uniform. One day Big Dung ran toward her, almost got under her umbrella, and caught the straw girl by surprise. In great excitement, Big Dung then ran back and reported that the girl was so unbelievably pretty, that in comparison our Youth League Branch secretary could only be described as a piece of spicy chicken wing. Puppy Zhao said, "If you feel that you are in love with a girl, you should first feel for your penis; if it fails to erect, it means that you are most probably truly in love with her."

The second time we set our eyes on her, she was coming our way. Every one of us reached into our trousers, and confirmed that we were in love with the straw girl.

She might be a clerk, and was often seen walking about the plant obviously unoccupied. Her uniform was always neat and clean and she also had on a pair of white leather gloves, something that was not available in any of the stores in the world. The forty of us decided to tail her. This time no one was asked to be the sentinel; the forty boys had to work together as a team. They were trailing behind her: when she moved, they moved; when she stopped, the forty boys pretended that they were taking a cigarette break; when she entered the cafeteria, forty people would squat near the entrance. If you were ever so fortunate to have been followed by forty boys, God bless. After everyone died, we would turn into forty crows and perch on your tombstone.

Finally, she walked into the warehouse for rejects—she was a caretaker there.

One day I went to the cafeteria when the straw girl was

having lunch there. She had a small aluminum lunchbox and a pink-colored teacup with a beautiful design of grapes painted on it. It turned out that the pork hock with winter bamboo shoots I'd once enjoyed had been her lunch.

I didn't notice that one of her fingers was missing.

The workshop manager pointed his finger at us and said, "Damn, you boys don't even know how to operate the lathes properly, you produced nothing but rejects. Just watch out that you don't get your fingers into the machines, like the young girl at the warehouse for rejects."

All our heads turned toward him and we asked, "Did she lose her finger in the end?"

The manager replied, "She started out as a lathe operator and lost a finger in the operation."

That's really nothing. At the bearing factory, on average, lost fingers could fill up a bowl per year. Pretty or ugly, once your fingers were lost, everything became equal. That's really nothing; the fact that the straw girl had one of her fingers missing was not at all unusual.

Quiff got the movie tickets already—he meant to ask her for a movie night out—but in the end he gave the tickets to Toady Fang and me. He had a change of heart right before we were to leave for home, saying that he still wanted to invite her for the movie. Quiff was too damn romantic. He had my sympathy, so I returned the ticket to him. But the son of a bitch Toady Fang had lost the movie ticket. Quiff left with the only ticket in between his fingers, and no one knew what happened afterward.

The assembly plant was located on the outskirts of the city, an hour and half ride on the bicycle. My mother once said that men would become sterile if they rode the bicycle for more than two hours a day. I was hoping that I would become sterile so that I didn't have to worry about getting girls pregnant. I had no idea where to find contraceptives.

Of course, neither did I know where to find girls.

Plague brought a videotape from the video rental store run by his family. At his father's store, we had seen more than a hundred Hong Kong-made movies and two hundred X-rated movies; once in a while we got to see a few triple-X-rated movies too, but not in the store. We enjoyed those at his house, instead, and had to treat him dinner in exchange. On one or two occasions, the forty of us were all present to view the movies. I remember only that Bald Eagle went to the bathroom, locked it from inside and asked us to turn the volume up, and up some more. But the videotapes Plague brought in didn't work at all in the wintertime since we had all been frozen into forty snails, and we even wished to squat to pee. Plague's feelings were hurt and he explained, it's an all-female cast movie, something you have never seen before. What he damn meant was that there were no men in it.

Something that we had never seen before.

The videotape was like a sealed jar of braised pork, and we were like forty crows that were hungry for braised pork. Its dark and heavy presence seemed to have our imaginations completely locked down.

We were wandering the plant grounds in the afternoon when a hidden air vent came into view. It was on a small mound behind the welding workshop, camouflaged by clumps of dried grass. Through the broken wood slats of the blind that covered the vent, we saw a deep shaft. It was a place worth exploring and we decided to throw Mangy down for a look. Mangy cried out, "Would you damn stop pushing me, I beg of you! I will do it, just let me do it on my own, there is a ladder going down."

Mangy went down and shouted, "There is a passageway going somewhere, it's too dark here to see anything."

Those who remained at the entrance of the vent got curious. Mangy was no longer in sight, but his voice came out loud and clear. The most daring among us decided to go down to take a look, followed by the less daring ones. And finally, the timid ones who were jumping around behind the welding workshop to ward off the freezing cold decided to go down there, too. The shaft couldn't accommodate all forty people, so Mangy led those in front along the passageway, followed by the others, cigarette lighters flickering on one by one.

We found ourselves in an underground dance hall.

Every plant had its own dance hall. The dance hall for the assembly plant was located underground, its ground-level entrance right next to the gatehouse. It was always locked and had an old watchman standing by. We heard that the place would open only once a month and only to staff members.

Cat-Face found the fuse box; with a push of the lever, the lights in the corridor went on. When the other switches were turned on, the ceiling lights lit up as well. We stayed away from laser lights for fear of disturbing those who were upstairs. It was a rather warm place, with many chairs with man-made leather cushions and many thermos bottles and cups. Right in front of the dance floor stood a huge television of unknown size. On the DJ platform behind it were sophisticated sound equipment gadgets.

The forty of us got the chairs, sat down and smoked.

Spareribs said, "What damn puzzles me is why the workers were given metal chairs in the workshop while there are comfortable man-made leather-cushioned chairs sitting around."

In fact, the reason was quite straightforward. The man-made leather-cushioned chairs are for enjoyment and the metal chairs are for work. You are not supposed to relax and enjoy in metal chairs and work in leather-cushioned chairs. But once Spareribs raised the issue, I got a little confused as well. So, after sitting on metal chairs for a month in the workshop filled with dust and noise, you were allowed to come to the basement one night, sit on the leather-cushioned chairs, sip tea, listen to music and dance. You were satisfied with this kind of life. But we crows found this incomprehensible.

Plague walked to the DJ place, and after a few minutes of

tinkering, he took the videotape from his satchel, inserted it into the player and turned on the TV. Following seconds of screeching sound, a woman and another woman appeared on the screen. Plague turned to Impotent Yang and said, "Didn't you say that the bigger the picture the bigger the arousal effect? Well, you are about to enjoy a big one."

Plague turned down the volume to the minimum for fear of alerting the old watchman upstairs. The old guy was very sensitive to such sounds. But the low volume turned out to be a big problem for us. As we moved closer to catch the sound, we could only see part of the picture; but once we moved away, the movie became inaudible. This proved to be a very special lesson on physical hygiene, and as far as I could remember the forty of us had never been this quiet before. Our silence could have been mistaken for solemnity.

When the viewing was over, we turned all the equipment off and restored the dance hall to its original state. We didn't know what to do with the cigarettes butts on the ground, and later decided to leave them where they were. As we walked out of the passageway in total darkness, Number Two Devil constantly poked me from behind. I felt very uncomfortable with this man-to-man intimacy right after seeing the woman-to-woman sexual scene. Number Two Devil claimed that it was out of his control—so long as he couldn't release himself, the thing would stay erect, and once he was out he would try to calm it down by burying it in the snow.

As we climbed up on the ladder, Number Two Devil's thing got in the way, and the pain was so unbearable that he fell on the heads of those behind him.

For the rest of the day, none of us could walk straight-legged; we all went around with our hands in our pockets, backs hunched, furtive looks on our faces. No one cursed the cold anymore.

Eunuch ate himself into trouble.

Every day, Eunuch would sneak to the cafeteria at 11 o'clock, pull the steamer drawers out and look for things to eat. That was the time when the food in the lunch boxes was already warmed up and the air was filled with the enticing smell, while the workers were still working in hunger and no one was in sight.

We didn't dare to steal the food anymore, but Eunuch was the exception. He just couldn't care less. He must have had some kind of a glutton syndrome, since he couldn't last more than an hour without food. In contrast, he didn't seem to be interested in women at all—all he cared about was food.

We didn't know at the time that he stole other people's food every day. It turned out that he not only raided one lunchbox, he would open up all the lunchboxes and teacups and just eat whatever he pleased, like a bear. That day, he ate something he would never forget for the rest of his life—somebody had put laxatives in one of the lunchboxes.

Eunuch wiped his mouth and sat in the cafeteria. We forty crows were all eating our hearts out while Eunuch sat there with a satisfied smile on his face. It was like that every day. But on this day, as he was smiling he started burping and his eyes stopped blinking, then with his eyeballs protruding, he started retching. Big Fly slapped him on the head and asked him to stop making that disgusting sound. The slap apparently cleared whatever blockage was in his body, and from Eunuch's behind came a series of splashing sounds. In great fear, Eunuch asked, "What happened?"

No one bothered to respond—we were all eating. Eunuch tried to stand up and run to the toilet, but the laxatives were very potent, the minute he stood up things just burst out like a drain being cleared of a clog by a plunger. We couldn't continue eating. Suddenly, Eunuch tuned his head, stared at us and shrieked, "What happened?"

That happened to be the coldest day of winter. It was so cold that no one even wanted to use the toilet. We relieved ourselves at whatever place we found convenient and came inside right away. But we had to help Eunuch to the toilet, and the helpers fell on ice one after another. Eunuch continued screaming, "I don't want to go to the toilet—I want to go to the hospital!"

He had it right, because it turned out that he was dehydrated.

According to the weather report, this was the city's coldest winter in a hundred years. The temperature had dropped to minus nine degrees Celsius. My mother said if it went down to minus ten degrees, the rules and regulations of the plant stated that we could have a day off.

So, the temperature given by the weather bureau stayed at minus nine degrees.

One day, we saw two factory workers emerge from the air vent leading to the underground dance hall, holding videotape recorder and microphone in their arms. While Red Devil believed we should try to catch the thieves, Plague was of the opinion that we should mind our own business. Red Devil said, "Plague, you are such a damn fool, your fingerprints were in the dance hall, if you let them go you will certainly be arrested for their crime." Plague soon realized his mistake, and he ran toward the thieves and kicked one of them back into the shaft. Later, a police car arrived and someone covered in blood was lifted from the shaft. Plague was also led away in handcuffs.

Every time Plague's name was mentioned, we lamented the fact that we could no longer watch videotapes for free. Forty minus two, Plague now received the same treatment that befell Hog's Intestine.

Winter seemed to have mellowed the forty boys to the point of depression. But as to why, no one could give you a clear answer. All we know is that they certainly would have behaved differently if it were summer.

None of the factory cadres dared to order us around anymore; after all, we were the ones who had smashed the windows, crashed the wheelbarrow, caused the destruction of the storage shed, and were even involved in a homicide. Everybody was waiting for the advent of the winter vacation, us included.

But truth be told, we were a bunch of depressed souls.

One morning when winter vacation was approaching, we didn't enter the factory gate. Instead we went directly to the breakfast stand right outside the gate. The road was crowded with people on their way to work, and every minute or so someone would fall from their bicycle. Forty crows sat there quietly enjoying their soy milk and breakfast, watching people falling and trying to get up, as if watching a boring movie. The one who arrived last was Meanie Chun, on a rarely seen mountain bike, far superior to our big wheel Phoenix brand. Meanie Chun claimed that it was an 800-yuan bike (1 yuan equals to 0.15 US dollars), real cool stuff. He made turn after turn right in front of our eyes on his bike. After staring at him for a while, Four Treasure put down his bowl of soy milk, walked over and dragged Meanie Chun down from his bike. He then announced, "The bike belongs to me now."

The two of them tussled in the snow.

The rest of us soon jumped in, wrestled down Meanie Chun and buried his head in the snow. He burst out crying. Money Maker got on the mountain bike, and along with Cabbage Kid on his Phoenix, they headed south. We continued enjoying our soy milk while Meanie Chun wailed and cursed. About half an hour later, Money Maker came back on the Phoenix with Cabbage Kid in the back. Cabbage Kid said, "The mountain bike was indeed damned valuable, it commanded 400 yuan. But what are we to do with the 400 yuan?"

There was a tin-roofed Wenzhou saloon not far from the factory, and we decided to have a good time there. So we said to Meanie Chun, stop your damn crying, we will at least let your small head enjoy a professional cutting and the rest of us will enjoy the full treatment.

Meanie Chun responded by saying, "Damn you, that bike is worth at least 500 yuan. Had I known that you were going to sell it, I would have given you the certificate, as well."

You see, Meanie Chun was not a guy without merit, in spite

of being mean. And we spared him from the harshest treatment exactly because of this saving grace of his.

We couldn't figure out why the tin-roofed Wenzhou saloon would set up business at this desolate place with no residents nearby. When we pushed the door open, we really scared the three girls who had just gotten up. They looked rumpled, and wore no makeup.

The room was fully equipped; congee was still cooking on an electric stove. The minute Bulky Five walked in, he tripped and tipped the congee pot. They said, "It's OK, it's OK, it doesn't really matter." We demurred, asking how they could manage to do forty haircuts on an empty stomach? So we sent Bulky Five to buy twisted crullers for them.

"You mean it? Forty haircuts?"

"Of course," we replied.

"In that case, we will go ahead and boil the water first." The girls were apparently pleased. One proceeded to boil the water, and the other two started putting on makeup.

The room was too small for all of us, so only a dozen or so were inside, with the rest waiting outside. Fortunately, we were used to exposure to extreme cold; plus, the thought of enjoying a haircut soon also brought warmth to our hearts.

At this time, a middle-aged man showed up at the hair salon on his bicycle, and he wanted to go in. We stopped him and asked why he was here. This middle-aged man replied cockily, "I am here for a haircut." We said, "Then you have to wait at the end of the line for your turn." The middle-aged man wouldn't take that for an answer. He stretched his neck in the direction of the store and called out, "Xiaoli!" We immediately grabbed him.

When he returned to where he parked his bicycle, the bike was no longer there. He started shouting, "Someone stole my bike!" We said we didn't see anyone stealing his bike, and weren't even sure he had even come in on a bike. He paused for a while, shook his head and walked away, probably thinking that this must be a dream.

His bike was actually taken by Fatso Huang for Meanie Chun. Although it was an old one, any bike was better than no bike.

While we were smoking outside, we heard a loud scream from Hao Bi, followed by shrieks of the girls. Fancy Pants ran out and announced with excitement, "Go in there quickly and take a look, Hao Bi just had a Mohawk haircut."

It was not the work of the girls, but us. Seeing Hao Bi in the mirror, the three girls burst out laughing. Hao Bi said, "Damn, every one of you will have the same style as mine, or I will set this shed on fire." We said, "That's not fair, the girls were not at fault. So what, Mohawks for all of us."

When it was my turn to sit by the washbasin, the Wenzhou girl was very tender; she poured shampoo on my head and worked my hair with her fingernails, hot water dripping down along my hair. She spoke with a heavy southern accent, and I closed my eyes, fantasizing that she was the girl I liked, and her hands were giving me gentle massages in fantasy and in reality, working as gently as if there were a huge scar on my skull.

Triangle Iron, Old Bandit and I were sitting on the three folding chairs at the same time, and the three girls immediately started working on our hair. A group of young men with Mohawk hairstyles were standing in the back. I would look just like them in no time, and probably would be like them forever.

Carrying a Girl on the Back to Mozhen Township

She was exquisitely beautiful, the most beautiful waitress I had ever seen in my life. She was as pure as the wonton soup that was just brought up to your table, and as innocent as a lily bouquet. Judging from her looks, she seemed to be around the same age as us, seventeen or eighteen years old at most. Even many years later, the memory of what happened then still haunts me and pains me to no end.

One day, eight of us skipped class and went mahjong playing at Big Fly's place. We played in two groups, four to each group. After playing straight until 7 o'clock in the evening, we all got very hungry. In the past, Big Fly's girlfriend would cook some noodles for us, but not this time, since she had just broken up with Big Fly. We had had enough of her noodles and believed that it was time for Big Fly to try something else as well, so we decided to eat out. Of course, Big Fly was still feeling down for being jilted.

We bicycled to the restaurant at the street corner. There were only a few customers inside, and only half of the ceiling lights were on, with the others kept off. We chose seats in the dark on purpose and asked the waitress to turn on the ceiling lights, which like spotlights on a stage shone directly on the eight of us. Fancy Pants was the big winner that day, so he was the one to make the order. He was wearing a black armband because his grandfather had just passed away. We superstitiously believed it was this black armband that had made him the big winner.

Fancy Pants ordered scrambled eggs, sautéed vegetables and tomato soup, the most inexpensive, ordinary home-style dishes. There were differences of opinion when it came to beverage orders. Big Ass wanted beer, Yellow Hair believed that having beer in winter was not good for your health and we should order rice wine instead; Big Fly would like to have Chinese vodka, a much stronger liquor, on account of the terrible mood he was in as he had lost not only his girlfriend but also money in the game. An argument ensued. The waitress suggested, "Why don't you order a bottle each of what you like first?"

We didn't notice her before because the light was on us. I said, "You are so pretty."

Big Ass put the menu down, stood up and took a good look at her and said rather seriously, "You look like a movie star, a Japanese movie star."

She stepped back a little, like a rabbit that had just seen the world for the very first time.

There are two kinds of beauty. The first kind might cause you to leave your senses, to babble and give you the urge to get close to it no matter what. The other kind would make you feel speechless, and you would lose command of your limbs. The first one is more like having a row, and the second one is more like having a physical fight. While she waited on us by the table, we began to melt away, and every gulp of drink we took would make our hearts pound. I had encountered pretty waitresses before—I would order beer after beer just to get them to come to me as many times as possible. But they were not as beautiful as she was; I had a hard time holding onto my chopsticks and they fell to the floor.

The only one who didn't fall for her was Big Fly. He said dismissively, "Is this the first time you ever came across a girl?" At this moment, Big Fly's heart had no one else but his former girlfriend. He might find room for this waitress with the passage of time.

Big Fly said, "Fancy Pants, you were really hot today. Take

off your mourning armband when we continue playing after dinner."

"In fact, I have another armband in my satchel. If you are not totally convinced, why not try wearing it for a change," Fancy Pants replied.

Fancy Pants' grandfather had penile cancer and died a terrible death. We all know that cancer might occur to any part of one's body, but it is really horrible to have cancer on the penis. Big Ass's mother was a nurse, and he claimed that the cancer was mainly caused by unsanitary habits—that part of the body needed to be washed often and thoroughly. Mangy asked, "What do you mean by 'thoroughly'? " Big Ass said, "Next time when we take a bath at the pesticide plant I will teach you how."

As we harangued about penises and cancer, the girl acted as if she hadn't heard anything at all, even though similar topics almost always made even the most serious girls from our technical school giggle.

Fancy Pants said his grandpa, who weighed only about forty kilos at the time of his death, had told him in relief that he could finally be together with Fancy Pants's grandma again.

"Sharing a bed in life, sharing the same burial ground in death," Yellow Hair sighed. "Do you know that the correct pronunciation of the character 衾 is *qin* and not *nian*?"

"Hats off for the scholar."

"Where was he buried?"

"Where else but Mozhen Township, where the public cemetery is. The place was so far away and the road was under repair at the time that when we'd finally arrived after a bumpy, hour-long bumpy jalopy ride, we had almost missed the noon burial deadline."

"I propose a toast to your grandpa," Big Fly said.

We had no more wine, so the girl brought us another bottle of rice wine. She then left to clean another table. The clashing and banging sounds became quite loud in the restaurant. Was it about to close? It seemed to be the case. There is no future for any restaurant that closes at eight in the evening. All the waiters and waitresses looked weary and lethargic as if they were also cancer patients, except her. She looked like a radiantly dazzling fairy wielding her magic wand in slow motion.

She became the topic of our conversation.

"She is really beautiful, and could be a trophy girlfriend."

"But she's just a waitress of the service industry."

"Hell! Your girlfriend is none other than a worker at a sulfuric factory who works on three shifts, whose complexion was as pale as someone who just climbed out of a coffin, and who are you to look down upon a waitress?"

"They are all out-of-towners."

"Ai JiMa (a Japanese actress) is also an out-of-towner."

"She is much more beautiful than Ai JiMa, just a bit less so than Joey Wong (a Hong Kong actress)."

"Should we take action? Which one is ready to act?"

"I have a girlfriend, Xiaoli, already, she would kill me if she finds out that I am seeing another girl."

"My girlfriend, Xiaoqian, would do the same if she finds out that I am unfaithful."

"Xiaoqian would have you castrated."

...

Among the eight of us, four had girlfriends already, and among the other four, Big Fly just broke up with his girl, and he was in no mood to date other girls, probably except Joey Wang. Fancy Pants's grandpa had just passed away, and it would be unseemly for someone wearing a mourning armband to date girls. Squinting Eyes and I were the only ones left.

Big Fly said, "Why don't you draw lots?"

We settled the matter by tossing the cap of a beer bottle, and Squinting Eyes won. I didn't protest the result, because I had long had my eyes set on the daughter of my literature teacher. It is true that I was awed by the waitress' beauty, but it might be an attraction confined to that particular time and place, and I couldn't say for sure if my fascination would last until tomorrow.

She was so beautiful, it would surely take more than one day for us to go steady.

The other seven people were staring at Squinting Eyes. Heavens, such an impossible winner. He was one of the only three students with glasses in our class, and not only was he near-sighted, but he also suffered from stigmatism. There were fuzzy black hairs over his upper lip that he refused to shave, as if preserving them added extra interest. His was a face covered with ulcered pimples, with glasses always slipping toward the end of his nose. He was a Communist Youth League member, and the reason we asked him to skip classes and play mahjong was to use his political background to spare us trouble. But we were a bunch true to our word, and we asked him, "Strike up a conversation with the girl. Do you need us to stage a fight for the girl and let you emerge as a winner who came to her rescue?"

"This is not going to work. You cannot take her away directly from the restaurant—you have to wait until the end of her shift."

Squinting Eyes was hesitating. He last dated a girl of a higher class who was rather plain-looking, but he spent all his savings on that girl in just one date, and that had been a hang-up for him ever since. You might find yourself in love with different girls at different times: pretty ones and plain ones, smart ones and not-so-smart ones, rich ones and poor ones, but you have to take the risk at least once on the most impossible ones, say, the daughter of a military commander.

Squinting Eyes decided to jump on this opportunity. Big Fly was the only one who sneered on the side. Big Fly had never had a high opinion of Squinting Eyes, and he didn't believe any girl would fall for such a fool.

"Why not give it a try, just for the fun of it? After all, she's merely a waitress." Squinting Eyes so comforted himself.

It was very cold at nine o'clock at night. Instead of going back to mahjong playing as originally planned, we now had to wait here in the wind. All for the sake of Squinting Eyes? No, it was not worthwhile, not at all. Perhaps we merely were interested to find out if she would fall for him, weren't we? We shivered in the wind. Squinting Eyes took out a cigarette, but the flickering light of the cigarette lighter proved to be no match for the blowing wind. Big Fly finally succeeded and we all huddled over to light up. Two drunkards came out of another restaurant nearby, and one stooped to vomit. The other one moved his motorcycle over, put the vomiting one on the back, and sped away, without even bother to put on his helmet.

"I would like to get a motorcycle when I graduate from high school," Yellow Hair murmured.

"With your spend-money-like-water girlfriend you would be lucky to hold on to your bicycle for the rest of your life," Big Ass responded sarcastically. "Why the hell did you insist on dating a girl who works in hotels? I suspect that she is also dating other boys. You bought her cosmetics, but what about her clothing, her shoes, and her jewelry?"

Yellow Hair said, "Shut up."

"Have you succeeded in sleeping with her? Or you are a big sucker?"

"I am not like you who enjoy smelling sulfur—you like the odor so much that it gives you your daily sense of security."

"F--k you."

Big Ass got angry—he found any mockery of his girlfriend, Xiaoli, who worked at the sulfur factory, most unbearable. That happened to be his raw nerve, but also our source of fun. He threw away his cigarette butt and said, "Why don't you morons stay here and wait. I am leaving."

Big Fly asked, "What about the game of mahjong?"

Big Ass said, "Didn't you see that I am in a rage now? The hell with mahjong." He got on his bike and soon disappeared in the shadows beyond the reach of the streetlight.

Rather like a girl, this asshole often left us in anger. We really didn't care that much about his presence or absence, since we knew that he would come apologizing with a pack of cigarettes in hand after a few days.

The girl came out. She had on a white ski jacket that covered her knees, and a red knit cap. It was a carrot-looking lovely cap, marking an arc on her forehead.

The six of us blocked her way, while Squinting Eyes hid himself in the back. Yellow Hair said, "Young girl, we are not bad guys, can we be friends? Let me start, my name is Zhang Weijun, nicknamed Yellow Hair."

Fancy Pants said, "I am Li Ning, the same name as the famous gymnast, my nickname is Fancy Pants."

Mangy said, "I am Lai Ning, same as the other Lai Ning, I'd rather keep my nickname to myself."

I told her, "My name is Lu Xiaolu."

Big Fly only said, "Hmm."

This time she didn't step back, neither did she cry for help. She looked at us seriously, lowered her head for a while, probably considering how to respond to our request. Yellow Hair assured her, "Don't worry, we just want to be friends with you. You work here and we often have our get-togethers nearby. Can we ask you out sometime? You have nothing to worry about; we are all class of '89 students of the tech school, majoring in instrument maintenance, with verifiable IDs."

The girl said, "Not tonight though—I need to go back home because my mother is sick."

"No problem, no problem. We can take you home. It would be too conspicuous if we all go with you, let Squinting Eyes do you the honor. Squinting Eyes, come forward, why hide yourself in the back? Look, he wears glasses, a truly trustworthy fellow; he is also the branch secretary of the Youth League. Squinting Eyes, show her the League logo on your clothes."

She seemed surprised. "You really want to accompany me home?"

Squinting Eyes gave her a positive response.

She said, "In that case, I am truly grateful."

It all went very smoothly. But we couldn't let our guard down yet. Once we had tried the same scheme on a girl, and she led Mangy directly to the Civil Defense Force.

"Where do you live?"

"Mozhen Township."

We were all taken aback. My goodness—Mozhen Township, the remote town where the cemetery is. According to Fancy Pants, the road was still under repair, and there would be no streetlights for that type of road. Heavens, wouldn't it be nice if we were a bunch of hooligans. But I doubted if even hooligans would be ready to commit crimes in Mozhen Township on a freezing cold night like this ...

"It's about thirty kilometers from here, right?" Squinting Eyes started wavering.

"Twenty-seven kilometers," Fancy Pants corrected him; he then turned towards the girl. "Do you go back home on bike or by bus?"

"There are no buses running at this late hour, so I can only ride my bike. My mother is sick," the girl said. "I have a place in town, but today I have to get back to Mozhen Township."

We huddled to the side to put Squinting Eyes at ease.

"Pick up your speed a little and you should get there in less than two hours. The road condition is not that bad and the section under repair is not long; it's right by the town border. This is a godsend! If you have escorted the girl home on the bike for twenty-seven kilometers in the dark night of winter, she would be your girlfriend for sure, or at least she would never forget you for the rest of her life. Just take a look at your sorry self; no woman besides your mum will ever remember you. This is a once-in-a-lifetime opportunity for you, and an honor for the school and the Youth League. If Big Ass were here, he would surely have fought you for the opportunity."

Stretching his neck over our shoulders, Squinting Eyes said to her, "No problem, I will escort you!"

The girl cried out, "Someone stole my bike!"

It had been left at the entrance of the restaurant but was gone now. She was almost in tears. I was about to suggest that she could borrow the ladies' bike idle at Big Fly's place when Squinting Eyes volunteered in a semi-trance, "No problem, come ride with me to Mozhen Township."

This was even better, come to think of it. Riding with a girl on a bike for twenty-seven kilometers, in a deep winter night, passing expanses of uninhabited areas, lined on both sides by slopes of half-hidden tombstones glistening in moonlight … wouldn't this experience rival that of a triathlon race? She sure would remember you for the rest of her life, whether you won the race or not. I became rather envious of Squinting Eyes. I had no clear idea of how long twenty-seven kilometers was—I only knew that she was so very beautiful, and if possible, I would like to carry her on my bike for two hundred and seventy kilometers or even longer. But I lost the bottle cap toss and I had no one to blame but myself.

They were about to be on their way. Squinting Eyes's bike was in such a bad shape, I had to lend him my Emmelle variable-speed mountain bike. The girl sat in the back, and Squinting Eyes had one foot on the pavement and the other one pushing the pedal hard. I said, "Use the third gear, stupid." As they moved unsteadily away, the girl put her arms around his waist. It was a most gentle gesture. Squinting Eyes must be melting.

"Can the stupid ass make it?" asked Big Fly.

"All I know is that the stupid ass is lucky with girls," Yellow Hair remarked. "Big Fly, you will regret it. By next week you will forget your former girlfriend, only to watch the stupid ass gloating."

Big Fly admitted, "I am already having second thoughts. But I have no intention of dating a girl from Mozhen Township, no, not at all."

It is true that people of our town tend to believe that girls of Mozhen Township (young men and all others included) are not clean. After all, it is a small town surrounded by cemeteries, a town people would visit only when there was a death in the family. Can you visualize a future son-in-law carrying cigarettes and wines walking past the tombs to visit his future in-laws? Or a bridegroom in Western suit from Mozhen Township walking past the tombs to receive the bride? In short, those images give you goose bumps. And we were a superstitious bunch.

"What if Squinting Eyes died on the road?" I asked.

Fancy Pants said, "That wouldn't happen. There are houses along the road and there is also a police station. He could cry for help and show people the League logo. So long as he stays the course, there is a good possibility that she could become his girlfriend. In fact, there is nothing wrong with girls of Mozhen Township, especially a beautiful-looking one like that."

Things are always like that—it is hard to say for sure if you are the winner or loser.

There were only six of us now, not enough to play mahjong in two groups. Fancy Pants wanted to go home, and so did I, so we went our own ways at the restaurant. I was feeling a bit down. Squinting Eyes and I were heading in the same direction, and I would have had no problem catching up with him on his jalopy. But I didn't want to do that. As I said before, I was a bit envious of him, and I didn't want to see her arms clutching Squinting Eyes' waist, even less on a bicycle that was mine. After everyone was gone, I stayed behind near the restaurant and smoked a cigarette, and only started on my way home after I figured that they were well on their way.

I lived on the outskirts of the town, and it was on the bridge outside of town I saw Squinting Eyes coming in the opposite direction. I asked, "What's the matter? Where is the girl?"

Squinting Eyes sighed. "On second thought, I think girls of Mozhen Township would bring nothing but bad luck."

"Bad luck or not, you have to escort her home, right?" I said.

"What's the point of courting someone who could only bring bad luck? Besides, I don't think she is that beautiful to begin with. She was forced upon me by you bastards, you people just want to see me making a fool of myself. Damn you," Squinting Eyes replied.

However foolish one may be, after being tricked enough times one eventually wises up. It seemed that Squinting Eyes had gotten smarter. But he was still a stupid ass.

I asked him, "Where is the girl?"

"At the other end of the bridge. I asked her to find a taxi and she agreed," Squinting Eyes answered.

"You swine," I cursed him. "Where would she find a taxi driver willing to go to Mozhen Township in the dead of night?"

I dragged him down off my mountain bike, got on it myself, and found her by an electricity pole at the other end of the bridge. She was covering her face with her hands and jumping up and down, huffing out white smoke. She didn't look as someone who had suffered embarrassment or humiliation. I stopped in front of her in seconds by hitting the brake hard; the bike made a sharp clacking sound. Very cool. I said, "I would like to introduce myself again. My name is Lu Xiaolu; you might as well forget the stupid ass who dropped you. I will take you to Mozhen Township."

"Thank you," she said.

I took off my scarf and put it on her. I knew that this would be a very hot ride for me and a cold one for her. I said, "Under one condition, though. After we arrived at Mozhen Township, you have to let me sleep over at your place. I don't want to bike back at three o'clock in the morning all by myself. I am not that silly."

With pleasure she replied, "No problem! We have a big house, a storied building!"

So, let's go.

Christmas Eve of 1991

B roody was a student of the Textile Academy. We all knew that eighty percent of the students of that school were female, while students of the Textile Vocational School that shared the same campus with the Technical School were a hundred percent female, an exact opposite of the student composition of our school, the Chemical Engineering Technical School. According to the popular saying, "Men should stay away from the chemical industry, and women should stay away from the textile industry," our two student bodies seemed to share the same sorry lot, but girls of that school didn't seem to care for us.

Broody was a friend of Big Fly. As to how they met, they most likely came to know each other through dance. Big Fly was a male dance partner, but Broody would kill me if she should be described as a female dance partner, since she merely loved dancing and wouldn't do it for money. She had been unhappy at the prospect of working in a textile factory after graduation. Her social background almost ruled out the possibility of her joining the administrative staff, so she seemed destined to work in three shifts among countless noisy machines and eventually yell when speaking. Luckily, she had a big voice to begin with. One day before Christmas, she stood in front of our school and shouted, "Show your face, Big Fly!" Eight people with the same nickname from six different classes of our Technical School all appeared. After checking it out among themselves, they figured that Broody was calling for the Big Fly of our class, and the other seven went back without making a protest, leaving Big Fly standing there alone.

"How come there are so many Big Flies in your school?" Broody asked.

"I have no idea, but I was the first one with that nickname. Damn it, too many men have 'Fly' in their names," replied Big Fly.

"We don't have any male students with that character in their names," Broody said.

"Even rats of your school are female," Big Fly retorted.

"You are a fraud. I liked you because of your name, and now there are so many men with the same nickname," Broody explained.

"This shows how little you understand men," Big Fly insisted.

"I have the feeling that I no longer like you as much now," Broody said.

At those words, Big Fly became panicky. Broody was a pretty girl, with big eyes and lips ready to pout at any time. And she was the only girl, or to be exact, the only age-appropriate girl, who was willing to have anything to do with Big Fly that the whole year.

Standing in front of the school, Big Fly looked around, felt all his pockets, scratched his head, and finally said to Broody, "Wait a minute here. I will go get some money and treat you to a cup of hot chocolate." It just so happened that I was on my way to school at the time. Big Fly pulled me to a stop, saying, "Give me back the five dollars you owe me from last time." I actually had no monetary problems with Big Fly and had never lost money to him in mahjong playing, either. But upon seeing Broody, I immediately understood what was going on and swallowed back all my questions. I gave him the only ten-yuan bill I had in my pocket, and the bastard Big Fly just took it all without a word. So I asked to be treated as well, Big Fly agreed, and we all went together.

The three of us sat in the store, feeling the boiling hot plastic cups and chatting. We had treated many girls for drinks here, cold fruit juice in summer or hot chocolate in winter. They were all sweet drinks, tasty and reasonably priced. But if you came here on a daily basis, or you planned to treat a bunch of them for drinks, you would be bankrupt.

Broody started by saying that it would be Christmas tomorrow. I corrected her that it was Christmas Eve and not Christmas. Big Fly laughed out loud because Broody often got the dates confused. She gave me a hard look and continued, saying that the Textile Academy had organized a dance party. Broody, the best female dancer of her class and the indisputable dance queen, having mastered quick- and slow-stepped jitterbug, needed a male partner. The female cadres of the student association had grabbed the few boys available at the Textile Academy; Broody, who was destined to work in shifts in the workshop, was forced to find a partner outside the school. And Big Fly was the only good male dancer of the right age she could find.

I didn't know much about dance or the world of dancing; I was crazy about video games and mahjong. If a girl was willing to dance with me I would certainly be ready to seriously learn my steps. Unfortunately, there were none.

Big Fly chose to step back, a misjudgment of the situation that had happened to him more than once. He said Li Xiao of our school was a good dancer, too, and she could try him. Broody said that Li Xiao looked older than his age, with his unshaved stubble and wrinkled forehead, and he risked being expelled by her teachers as an unemployed youth.

I chimed in, "Big Fly, don't be so modest. You are a very good dance partner, even for much older women." He gave me a kick under the table.

Annoyed, Broody asked, "Big Fly, are you coming or not?"

Big Fly said, "Of course, of course I am coming."

"So, what's the point of mentioning Li Xiao? You fool," Broody responded. "Li Xiao is in love with a girl from the Finance School, so he would never agree to spend Christmas at the Textile Academy," I interjected. Broody gave me a dirty look and decided to drop me from her invitation list because of my slip. Although I was not good at dancing, I was good at karaoke. Now by offending her I had lost my invitation and would most probably spend Christmas Eve at home with my dad.

Before leaving, Broody patted Big Fly's shoulder and said, "Six thirty tomorrow night. I will kill you if you don't show up." Turning to me, she added, "Damn, Lu Xiaolu, you might as well spend Christmas at the Finance School." Pointing at the hot chocolate, she then complained to the waitress, "It tasted terrible! Was it chocolate or Chinese medicine?" Afterward, she jumped on her bike and lost from sight.

Big Fly and I stayed behind to finish our hot drinks. But after Broody's complaint, I felt somehow that the hot chocolate of this store indeed tasted like Chinese medicine. I had been numb and I needed a girl to sharpen my senses, and help me to tell good drinks from bad ones. I said to Big Fly, "You should've treated Broody ice cream instead." Big Fly said that Broody's short temper was caused mainly by irregular periods, which could only be made worse by having ice cream in the winter, and he didn't want to take that risk. I said, "Wow, she would even share that information with you. But why do you like a girl with irregular periods?"

Big Fly finished his hot chocolate, stuck his tongue out to clean up any residual drink around his mouth, and asked me, "Damn, when you fall for a girl, do you rush to find out from her if she had menstruation problems first?"

I was struck by boredom. Yes, this coming Christmas was doomed to be a boring one. There was a school party last Christmas, with karaoke included in the program. But my microphone was taken away when I was only halfway through my song. A fight among students for the only two microphones ensued, and the grudges were so deep between factions that the fighting continued off and on into this year as well. It was unlikely that the school would organize similar activities in the future.

As for Big Fly, he was a born dancer and had been dancing ever since he was a child. He would be in his element in an art troupe. Unfortunately, he grew up to be a stocky boy with short limbs, more like a metalworker. God blessed him with Christmas every day, but never gave him a real gift. Now he spent his spare time at Springtime Ballroom: when men were not in demand he would act as a bouncer, and when there was a shortage of men, he would fill up as a hired dance partner, holding girls close to him in social dances. He could earn about a hundred yuan at the ballroom, with sixty yuan going to his stingy dad for food and the other forty going in his own pocket. He would work twice as hard during the summer and winter breaks to earn enough for tuition.

Big Fly and I were fair-weather friends. For a while I also wanted to make money at the ballroom, but Big Fly was reluctant to take me in. He said I would get bored since I didn't really care for dancing and liked merely the money part. True, I liked merely the money part. If I could make a hundred yuan, plus the other hundred I swindled from my dad, I would pass as a rich guy in our Tech School and date girls from the Finance School. But in exchange, I would have to sell myself to Springtime Ballroom, to work there as a bouncer or a lewd dance partner. God blessed me with Christmas gifts, but not Christmas. What an irony.

Of course I couldn't date girls from the Finance School, because all of them would work as accountants after graduation, a profession that was several rungs higher than my future employment. I might as well try my luck with girls from elite high schools, my reasoning being that some of them were bound to fail at the college entrance exams and if they couldn't find work as high-school graduates, their situations would be even worse than mine.

When school was over the next day the weather became terrible, dark and gloomy at first, followed by freezing rain. When I hurried home, Big Fly was long gone. The street scene was more or less the same, not decorated with colorful ribbons or lanterns as when we celebrated the National Day or the Spring Festival, nor were there wishing-well posters. It was a misty gray and ice-cold Christmas Eve. Why would people choose to celebrate important holidays in such terrible weather? Christmas, New Year, Spring Festival, and the recently arrived Valentine's Day.

I stopped at a clothing store on my way home to browse the latest fashion. A washed-denim jacket caught my eye; it had a white fake-fur collar and a knitted design on the back. I felt it with my hand. I tried it on at the urging of the middle-aged saleslady, and it did make me look cool. After being told that it was four hundred yuan, I took it off, cursed and was ready to leave. The curse got me in trouble and she refused to let go of me. Two men soon joined in and confiscated my satchel. I sat down at the store entrance and started negotiating with them. After haggling, the price was slashed from four hundred to one hundred and eighty, but I had to pay an extra twenty yuan for the curse I threw at the sales lady, so the final price was two hundred. They agreed to wait for me to get the money from home, but if I failed to show up before their closing hour they would throw my satchel into the river.

I was hit with a sense of sadness when I had the denim jacket and satchel in hand, as if I had just been blackmailed. As much as I liked the jacket, I should not have agreed to buy it under duress. I had to steal the two hundred yuan from home. Although my mum probably wouldn't give me a hard time for my action, stealing her money for this lousy deal still bothered me no end. Freezing rain continued falling while I rode my bicycle aimlessly around town, until my raincoat had a thick layer of ice buildup on it. Then I ran into Big Fly in front of the Springtime Ballroom.

He had on a rather thin sweater with worn-out sleeves, clutching in hand an unopened pack of Red Pagoda Mountain cigarettes. I pushed back the hood of my poncho and asked him, "You didn't go to the Textile Academy?"

Dejected, he told me, "I couldn't get away—there is also a

Christmas Party at the Springtime Ballroom tonight. I meant to leave at six for Broody, but the boss wouldn't let me go."

"Why don't you just walk away?" I asked.

"If I leave without permission, I will lose this job for good, and this is the only damn job I have to keep the family going," replied Big Fly.

"What about Broody? She will kill you," I said.

"Could you take my place for a while?" Big Fly asked.

"Your boss doesn't even know me, how could I replace you?" I questioned.

"I don't mean here. I am asking you to keep Broody company for a while. At least you know the 'four steps' I taught you before. Once the initial segment is over, I will see if I can leave at eight and take over. If she still wants to kill me later, I only have myself to blame." Big Fly opened up the pack of cigarettes, put one in his mouth and handed me the rest.

I glanced at him with sympathy. Poor Big Fly. His sense of responsibility would never allow him to walk away from his post, not even for a second. He was standing there, smoking in the icy rain, trembling with cold, and looking aimlessly around when I left him. And then, after a pat on the head by his boss, he went back in with the cigarette dangling from his lips.

Big Fly once told me that Broody's life was a miserable one. She might look tough and aggressive on the outside, but she was an outcast in school. Last year, she had been punished for using abusive language toward her teacher, and this year she again suffered a public humiliation by being beaten up on the Textile Academy campus by several girls from another school. All she wanted now was to leave the school as soon as possible and work in a factory in shifts. That was the lousy story I had heard often that year. Everyone was eager to leave where they were, whatever their next station might be.

With an empty stomach, I finally arrived at the Textile Academy after crossing four blocks. It was completely dark now. I parked my bike, shook the icy buildup from my poncho, and stuffed it into my satchel, so that I didn't have to show up with all that mess in front of Broody. I then put the denim jacket on and tied my cotton jacket on the sling of my satchel. I walked into the well-lit classroom building, which was crowded with people. Colorful ribbons were hung everywhere; it was a pity there was no Christmas tree in sight. The year was 1991, and there were no Christmas trees, period.

There was a karaoke party in one of the classrooms on the first floor, so I went in and asked for Broody's whereabouts. Many girls were in there, but I got no response. I again raised my voice and asked the same question, and a girl answered through the microphone, "Broody is dancing upstairs, on the fourth floor." I was about to step out when the same girl asked through the microphone, "Lu Xiaolu, come up and sing a song with me."

I didn't know the girl and had no idea how she got my name etched in her memory. She was pretty, a big-sister type of a girl, the type whose presence would invariably make me feel like I'd been struck on the head. I didn't even wait to find out her name before I readily took the microphone and sang the song "Yes or No" with her. "Are you really going to leave me this time, yes or no?" I sang those words full of emotion, as if I were really about to leave her. Hell, I would indeed leave her for Broody upstairs, but I was too emotionally attached to what I was singing. As our singing came to an end, the girl was so pleased that she asked me to sit down and have some snacks. I was hungry and finished almost half of her bag of snacks, and I also drank the water she offered. Finally I asked, "How did you come to know me?"

"I spent the last Christmas at your school and saw you singing—you have a nice voice."

"A fight ensued," I said.

"Yes, there was a fight," she said.

"Our school is known for campus fighting," I said.

"Yes, it's known for campus fighting," she said. "Our school has only occasional fights, among girls."

"That must be quite a scene," I remarked.

"Yes, quite a scene," she echoed.

We sang two more songs. As I said before, I was very good at karaoke. One of my hobbies was to use a recorder and learn all types of popular songs at home. I followed the ranking of popular songs on a weekly basis, learned all of them and waited for the limited opportunities to show off my skills. I don't think I stayed there for long, and it didn't seem to me that I did anything or said anything at all. The room was filled with girls, they took turns to sing solos, duets or group songs. The Christmas party atmosphere was growing. I even took the liberty of smoking a cigarette and no one complained. I asked the name of the big-sister-type girl.

She sounded somewhat lost, "Sima Ling."

That was a name with tremendous killing power. I now remembered that she was the girl of a fellow student in my school, only of a higher class and a known bully. Because of her, he had broken the skulls of several people already. God only knew why she was sitting here alone and spent Christmas by singing along with me.

"What time is it now?" I asked her.

"Almost eight."

I ditched her immediately and ran upstairs, shouting to her at the same time, "Don't let your idiot boyfriend know, or I would die a violent death!" Like a deranged kangaroo, I made a beeline up the stairs and arrived at the classroom converted into a dancehall as graceful waltz music played. Dancers crowded the floor, and a huge Christmas tree decorated with glistening cellophane was chalked on the black board. I found Broody under the chalk-painted Christmas tree.

She apparently had been crying, and her face looked a little swollen, dotted with tearstains, her eyes glazed. She was playing with a trinket out of boredom. She had dressed for the occasion in a pink down jacket, shiny patent leather shoes and a fuzzy head decoration. She was obviously disappointed that Big Fly didn't show up on the night she had planned so meticulously.

As soon as she caught sight of me at the door, she came running and asked me in a low voice, "Where is Big Fly?"

"He couldn't make it, but will probably show up later," I answered.

"Shit!" Broody cursed. "I have been so humiliated."

"Well, you know, he was held up at the Springtime Ballroom. If he chooses to leave on his own, he might lose the job for good. You know the unfortunate situation he is in—this is the only job that keeps him alive."

"There is no need to explain," Broody said.

"He asked me to take his place," I ventured. "I know how to dance the 'four steps.'"

"You are of no damn use," clenching her teeth, Broody dismissed me in a suppressed voice, "I have let the word out, and everyone knows by now that my partner tonight is Big Fly and not you."

"It's up to you. If you don't like the idea, I will go home. Maybe I will be hacked to death tomorrow."

Sizing me up and down, Broody realized that I actually was much handsomer and smarter-looking than Big Fly, and the reason I had looked shabby before was that I didn't have the denim jacket on, that's all. I had this special quality about me before I would be hacked to death. Broody suddenly declared, "Oh, the hell with it. After all, not that many people know who Big Fly is, and there are so many Big Flies in this world." She grabbed the collar of my denim jacket and dragged me into the classroom. The waltz music had just come to a stop, and many girls and their male partners turned to stare at me. With a deafening voice that really shocked my sense of hearing, Broody declared, "Big Fly, if you dare to be late again, the next time I will kill you."

You Are a Witch

In those days, girls all tried hard to impress people with their hairdos, such as big waves, small curls, ponytails, swimmer's short cuts and others, but no one dyed their hair. Hair dying became a fashion only much later, so late that they had probably all grown up by then.

But there was one girl who was born with a small cluster of white hair that had the same effect as what would be known as "highlighting" later. In those days, we had no idea what "highlighting" was. She was a student at the Number Eight Middle School, not far from our Tech School. Every morning she would join us in the army of bicyclists, and the string of white hair that hung from her right temple all the way to her shoulder had piqued our curiosity. In order to get a better look of her face, we usually stopped at a breakfast stand along the street for soy milk ahead of time, and waited.

She was a quiet beauty. But with the heavy influence of videos from Hong Kong, we preferred hot girls like Hu Huizhong, Li Saifeng, and Oshima Yukari. In short, the female police inspector kind. Wouldn't it be lovely that we were the ones beaten up by the beautiful policewomen and sent flying across the ground, with safety hooks in the back? The girl Noisy, who often hung out with us, was also a hot girl. When she was in a good mood she would allow us to touch her behind, but when she was in a bad mood she would kick our behinds instead, so we had no communication problems whatsoever. And yet, with this white-haired girl who refused to interact with us, none of our tactics seemed to be working.

There are two ways to enjoy soy milk. If you like it sweet, all you need to do is to add sugar to it; if you like the salty kind, you need sesame oil, soy sauce, sea weed, dried shrimp, chopped preserved mustard and chopped crullers—almost equivalent to a big dish. Quiff theorized, bad girls are like salty soy milk and good girls are like sweet soy milk. They taste different, but they are all soy milks. He then asked, "What about plain soy milk?"

"That will be your mother," Fancy Pants replied.

Our conversation while drinking soy milk went often like that; somehow this kind of nonsense put us all in a great mood, and lightened up our boring school life. For the rest of the day, our talk might shift to girls, money, or the three Dutch players in the Italian Series-A League.

Quiff was the one who had discovered her first, but Cat-Face disputed that, and claimed that he was the one who had really spotted her first. Quiff was one of us, a member of the good force on the Earth, whereas Cat-Face was one of "them." We often fought among ourselves like in the movie "Transformers," bringing havoc to the peaceful world. According to Quiff, he was sitting at the breakfast stand one day when the girl showed up unexpectedly. She parked her bike and ordered a bowl of sweet soy milk. Despite his efforts to get her attention, she didn't respond at all to the passes made by someone with a mouthful of ingredients of the salty soy milk, and she left on her bicycle right after she finished her drink. Quiff was the romantic kind, so he wanted to follow her, but there was still quite a lot of stuff in his bowl. As she left, he noticed the string of white hair on the side of her head, and the world had since been brightened up.

Cat-Face's story was similar. One day, as he was approaching the breakfast stand, he saw her leave the empty bowl on the table, take her satchel and go for her parked bike. He said he was still in awe when she walked by and her white hair almost touched his jaw due to overcrowding. As he saw her leaving in leisure, he tried to catch up on his bike, but it just so happened that he had a flat tire. Cat-Face stressed that this all happened before Quiff met her, and that he was the one who first crossed paths with her.

Whichever version is true, neither of them caught up with her, nor had they succeeded in striking up a conversation with her later.

Now as she rode past, a dozen of us sat at the breakfast stand like beggars with only two orders of salty soy milk. The owner of the stand was almost in tears. In a few seconds, she flitted past our eyes in a crowd, an image of a typical high school girl student in a rush to join others in morning sessions of self-study. In comparison, we Tech School students seemed too relaxed and too laid back, as we didn't need to prepare for the college entrance exam, nor did we need to look for jobs; jobs at the chemical plants would be waiting for us upon graduation. Life was so easy in our lousy school that there were no morning sessions of self-study, morning exercises, or even flag-raising ceremonies. We were truly a depraved bunch.

Big Fly let out the words, "Go after her."

We all got on our bikes and got on the road like a group of bats getting into action after dark. This was a road lined with stores on both sides. It was considered quite wide in the seventies, but it looked more like a crowded battleground in the beginning of the nineties, especially during rush hours when bikes took up almost all the spaces, including the pedestrian walks. Bicycle bells were heard everywhere and tires were rolling in whichever direction you looked. No cars dared to drive through here, except buses and night-soil trucks.

As we got on the road en masse, traffic came to a stop and people started complaining. There were people who needed to get to offices early to read newspapers and drink tea, or they might lose their bonus. Of course they were the kind of people about whom we couldn't care less. We zigzagged among them in pursuit of the string of white hair, like a bunch of fools who had too much turtle essence. Then we heard a scream from Fancy Pants.

Fancy Pants hated chasing after girls, and he joined the pursuit just so that he could catch up with us. Little did he expect that he would crash head-on into a bulky middle-aged man. The man fell onto a row of chamber pots lined up on the sidewalk for drying. He got back to his feet, grabbed Fancy Pants and slapped him. So we stopped the chase and returned to punch the man, instead. As a result of the commotion, we lost sight of the girl. The most popular girl in our circle was Noisy. She had shiny black hair, gorgeous features and she always smelled good. Every time I saw her she reminded me of a string of grapes that grew from the neighbor's yard over the wall and dangled in front of a group of wild boys; she was simply irresistible.

She was not dating any of us, just the most kind-hearted one among so many street girls. One day we caught her playing a game console in front of the movie theater all by herself, we chatted her up and she soon became one of us. She was more bohemian than the rest of us. We managed to hang on to a tech school, while she stopped going to school altogether. She spent all her time loitering and playing, and was the kind of girl Quiff called the salty soy milk.

"What do you mean white hair? You guys care about white hairs?" Noisy asked.

"A different kind of white, just a string of white, better looking than the white-haired witch," Quiff answered.

"I saw her first," Cat-Face claimed.

"Stop arguing, you two. Whoever succeeds in pursuit of her will be the real winner," Noisy declared.

"I am a better bicyclist. I will surely catch her first," Quiff said.

"Are you stupid or what, don't you understand me? I mean 'pursuit' and not 'catch up with her' on a bike. Of course, you are not totally wrong either, because damn, you first have to get on your bike and catch her," Noisy continued.

Hao Bi got excited, "If I managed to catch up with her, could I be declared a winner?"

Glancing at the prematurely gray Hao Bi who looked nothing but scary with his messy white hair flying in the wind while riding the bike, Noisy said, "I don't think you will catch her, and the idea that you should be paired with the same prematurely gray girl is a lousy one."

With some embarrassment Hao Bi confessed that he actually liked blonds.

After everyone left, Noisy asked me to escort her home. I told her, "None of them will really succeed. The Number Eight High School is a good one, and girls of that school would never agree to have any relationship with our Tech School."

"What did you say just now? Did you say relationship?" Noisy asked.

"Don't let your imagination run wild, what I meant was the relationship we have between you and me. But even limited relationship like this would be beyond their reach. They will not succeed and will only end up in big trouble if they try."

Noisy said, "You and Fancy Pants are the most arrogant ones in your group."

I nodded in agreement. For a while, this girl who hadn't had much schooling, who was known for her sharp tongue and ruthlessness, was my confidante of the opposite sex. She knew how to use those literary words, such as "arrogant," "gentle," "melancholic" and "introvert." Fancy Pants and I were arrogant, Quiff was gentle, Big Fly was melancholic and Cat-Face was an introvert. It went without saying that there were also the purely stupid ones, like Hao Bi and Hog's Intestine.

"Strange, why would you all fall for a white-haired girl? Does she look that chic?" Noisy asked.

I told her I didn't know, since I never had a good look of her. But I intended to catch up with her one of these days and find out. Noisy was a bit lost, but soon resumed her sunny outlook and said, "I will let you in a secret. I have a boyfriend now, an owner of a billiard room. I may not hang out with you guys for long, may you have fun in chasing after the white-haired girl."

It was my turn to feel lost. In fact, I liked Noisy and was ready to forget the white-haired girl if Noisy was willing to be my girlfriend. Too bad that she had found someone she loved. For a while I was even under the illusion that I would stay faithful to her for the rest of my life.

Then, the chase started.

The first one to chase her was neither Cat-Face nor Quiff, but Mangy. He was lucky that day because he saw the white-haired girl riding past him at high speed, before reaching the breakfast stand. Mangy was taken by surprise and he pedaled hard in an attempt to catch up. But he was a small and skinny guy and the only one in our class to ride a lady's bicycle. While riding with us, his bike looked more like a donkey among warhorses. As he rode past the breakfast stand, he shouted at Fancy Pants, "She is ahead of me!"

"Who?" Fancy Pants frowned and asked.

"The white-haired girl."

"Stupid ass." Fancy Pants chose to stay and enjoy his soy milk.

"I need to take a closer look; I didn't even see the white hair part." Mangy continued with his chase right after uttering those words.

The chase turned him into a troublemaker in the crowded but orderly bicycle traffic. First he scraped someone's handlebar, and as he lost his balance he slammed into a tree. Upon seeing him crash his bike from afar, Fancy Pants shook his head and commented to the stand owner, "His nickname is Mangy, and he is considered the most hopeless student in our Technical School."

The owner asked, "Why did he want to see the white-haired girl?" Fancy Pants' answer was, "They are all crazy."

Seeing Mangy show up at school with bruises on his, we all roared with laughter. At the time, the school was in the midst of a civilization campaign; firstly, smoking was banned, and secondly, we were asked to observe a dress code: students wearing denims were ordered to take them off and run around the classroom building in underpants. The school then checked our hairstyles and whiskers with all seriousness. At the age of seventeen or eighteen, we all had fuzzy hair growing above our upper lips, which the school considered inelegant; we were asked to shave them as whiskers. The general rule that applied to everyone was simple: no one was allowed to have any damn facial hair. I was most unlucky, since the use of my father's shaver had left me with bloody scratch marks all around my mouth. His shaver turned out to be more terrifying than kitchen knives. As we were driven crazy by those ridiculous rules, the sight of Mangy brought our minds back to the white-haired girl.

The next morning, a clean-shaven and handsome-looking bunch, with chins like chickens' behinds in a freezer, all sat at the breakfast stand for a glimpse of the girl.

As soon as she showed up, unlike the previous times, we all ditched our bowls immediately and started the chase. I was ahead of everyone else, but as I negotiated the crowded bicycle traffic, she seemed to be getting farther and farther away. Something was not right. I was riding a big-wheel Phoenix bike whose speed could match that of a truck on regular road surface, and I couldn't even catch up with a high-school girl. All the pedestrians were in my way, and all the people were trying to give me a hard time, just like teachers of my school. I pedaled hard, really hard, only to see Cat-Face ride past me.

I shouted, "I am rooting for you, Cat-Face!"

"The hell with you, stupid ass, you are only good for escorting Noisy home like a dog," Cat-Face said.

I was angry and tried to catch up with him and give his bike a hard kick. But with lightning speed, Cat-Face shot far ahead into the traffic. Big Fly caught up with me and said, still gasping for air, "Haven't you noticed that Cat-Face has a new bike?"

I noticed it only there and then; true, it was a brand-new Phoenix. I hope this fool didn't replace his bike because of the girl, or it would be such a waste, and his romanticism would put even Yang Guo (the hero of Jin Yong's popular martial art movie *The Legend of Condor Heroes*) to shame. I had to confess that his obsession had made me somewhat jealous. But shit, he dared to mock Noisy and me. It was true that Noisy was not that important to me; still, what right did Cat-Face have to mock me? Ignoring Big Fly, I continued my chase. From an alleyway about ten meters away, a night-soil truck suddenly stuck its nose out at full speed. It had its mission to accomplish and couldn't care less about people commuting between home and work. After collecting the stuff from one public toilet on this pleasantly cold morning, it would usually rush fearlessly to another one, like a drunkard, leaving drips of its goodies along the way. We all applied our brakes in a hurry, as if the truck were a monster. As I almost flipped over the handlebars, I saw Cat-Face smashing into the truck before he could even utter a scream.

In the days that followed, the pavement became unusually slippery as a result of the spring rain. People all wore hooded raincoats that made their faces unrecognizable. When having our soy milk in the morning, we often lamented the fate of the crazy Cat-Face, who was now hospitalized with a broken collar bone. Without him, the atmosphere seemed more peaceful; days of rain also seemed to have had a calming effect on us.

We kind of missed Noisy; we all knew she was in love now. According to Quiff, the billiard room owner might be rich, but he was a country bumpkin and had no taste, and he didn't even know how to play billiards. How could the owner of a game room not knowing the game!

Fancy Pants said to Quiff, "You are actually Noisy's favorite."

"Impossible," replied Quiff.

"Well, that's what she said to me herself. But you fancied the White-Haired Witch," Fancy Pants explained. She got this nickname ever since Cat-Face broke a collarbone because of her.

Quiff might be romantic, but he still found the latest revelation quite confusing. He was not that smart. Why is it that Noisy had her eyes set on him and not someone else, and why didn't she say so herself instead of letting Fancy Pants spoil the news? We all got confused. Fancy Pants said dismissively, "You wouldn't understand. There is only one Noisy in this world, but girls you fools chased on the road, be they white-haired or dark-haired, come in tens of thousands. Do you understand?"

Quiff fell into silence. Big Fly slapped the table and said,

"Fancy Pants, you know nothing, nothing at all. Noisy in fact has many boyfriends. She was never serious with any of us."

Now we all fell silent. At that time, someone came in, parked a bike, walked toward the shed of the breakfast stand and pushed back the hood of her raincoat, exposing a head of drippy hair. It was the witch. Under our stares, she swung her head and the string of white hair on her temple flung like a curved knife. She ordered a sweet soy milk.

We stopped our conversation about Noisy. The witch sat at a table next to ours and drank her soy milk slowly. The white steam from the bowl misted her eyes; she raised her head a little, but never cast her eyes our way. She looked so much like a martial arts specialist. After a brief daze, Quiff suddenly stood up, and sat down again; he acted as if his restless heartbeats had begun to affect his behind. The rest of us were more like a group of bandits rendered frozen by a kung fu master. She was a real beauty, a different kind of beauty; Noisy seemed vulgar and flighty next to her. I lit a cigarette for myself and started questioning if I should go after such a pure and serious girl; I started having second thoughts about her. Paying no attention to her surroundings, she finished her soy milk under our watch. She then stood up, paid the bill, got her bike and moved toward the road. All of a sudden she turned and said to us, "Stop following me. My father works for the public security bureau."

She was very serious. Fancy Pants waited until she was no longer in sight and said slowly, "Don't you feel bad about yourselves?"

When we were seventeen or eighteen years old, we had chased many girls. Every one of them, without exception, became panicky, as if they were about to fall into the hands of wolves. In fact, that was exactly our tactic. We often acted like a bunch of hooligans and tried to encircle the girls with our bikes. Once a girl got so scared she started to cry. Another time, we were outflanked by dozens of good Samaritans, who managed to get hold of the unluckiest one among us and tie him to a lamppost for the police.

This wasn't as fun as you'd think, and you get bored if you

play the same game too many times. Once you detected their expression of boredom, you would feel that you were like the truck that collected night soil. It would always show up in the morning, make its routine rounds when the air is clear, having no bad feelings about itself and feeling no shame.

One day, I went to see Noisy all by myself. She had an exaggerated, big-wave hairdo and looked at least five years older under the dingy light of the billiard room; her head seemed enveloped in a haze of smoke exhaled by others. I said, "The hairdo makes you look much older."

Seemingly indifferent to my comment, Noisy asked, "Any luck with the white-haired girl?"

"No, it turns out that we have come across a witch this time. Fancy Pants got slapped in the face. Cat-Face crashed into a night-soil truck in his chase and was hospitalized for a broken bone. Mangy rode into a tree, and Bandit made the mistake of following her into her school and was taken to the police station for hooliganism. None of them came to good ends," I told her.

Noisy had a good laugh.

I later asked her if she really cared for Quiff and her reply was a flat no. I told her that was what Fancy Pants told others and I merely wanted to check if it was true. Deep inside, I always believed that she liked me the most. Betraying a little impatience, Noisy warned, "My boyfriend will be back soon, so let's call it quits. He is a toughie and will beat your head off if provoked."

She seemed serious too as she said that.

"Oh, I don't mind, 'cause I'm a tough guy, too," I joked.

"Please, you are nothing but a ... young apprentice of class of '89 of the Chemical Engineering Technical School," Noisy said. "You will work as an apprentice at a factory, won't you?"

I got very angry. After those hurtful words, she took the cue and went back to mind the business, very much like a mistress of the billiard room. She had rapidly turned from grapes to raisins in my eyes and I had no choice but to leave. I felt somewhat sad at first, but soon recovered. I thought there was more than one Noisy in this world, and Fancy Pants was wrong: there was never just one Noisy. Even the present Noisy was merely half of what she was before, and she would continue to shrink in size, until she became someone who was no longer her old self. This sounds quite convoluted, doesn't it?

It was quite peaceful in the days afterward. We no longer chased the white-haired girl, and Noisy also stopped hanging out with us for fun. Even Cat-Face, a member of the enemy camp, was no longer with us. But the spiritual civilization campaign continued with great fanfare. We all had shaved our facial hair. They said that the more you shaved, the stiffer the hair would become, and by the age of thirty, it would be as hard as a nylon brush.

One day in early summer, we were loitering aimlessly around town. It was a very quiet afternoon. As the entrance of the Number Eight High School came into view, Hao Bi said out of the blue, "Do you still remember the white-haired girl? Her name is Zhang Yu, a classmate of my cousin who attends the same high school."

"What about her?"

"She is a high school senior, and according to my cousin, she intends to take the entrance exam and pursue college education. She's got good grades," Hao Bi said.

"Her father works at the public security bureau."

"No, she fooled you," Hao Bi continued, "her father is a teacher."

We all shook our heads and sighed. Hao Bi added, "Haven't you heard what had happened to Noisy? The fire that was in the news yesterday not only burned down the billiard room but also took the life of her boyfriend."

"F--k you." We were all surprised.

"We can all go and ask her to hang out with us again," Hao Bi said.

"Count me out," I said, "you may go on your own."

Then we heard the bell ringing and school was over. Students started leaving in twos or threes. We pushed our bikes into shaded areas on the side. Hao Bi suddenly cried out, "White hair, white hair!"

It was her again. The picture of her on a bike quickly went past us. No one said anything, nor did we plan to go after her. We were all scared to death of her. Only Hao Bi got very excited, as he always was. He was the most emotional guy among us, and he also hated his own guts the most. He jumped on his bike and asked us to join him in the chase. Quiff advised, "Don't, you might fall and die." But Hao Bi was already in hot pursuit, his prematurely gray hair flying like dandelions in the wind. Quiff raised his voice, "Stop the damn chase, didn't you hear me?" Hao Bi didn't hear him; he had actually caught up with her. He even turned back and whistled at her, the loudest whistle he'd ever given in his life.

"Get out of my way!" We all heard the girl's scream.

Traffic was light, and a truck carrying steel rods was going in the same direction at high speed, with more than three-meter-long rods hanging out of the body of the truck. The truck was going so fast and so close to them, I had the feeling that I would surely hear the sound of metal being crushed as the bicycles were dragged under the wheels of the truck. But I was wrong. As the truck drove away, the girl, looking dazed, was staring ahead of her, with one foot on the pedestrian walk. Then she let loose a loud guffaw. That was the last time I saw her, and the serious expression she wore before was no more. And I never saw Noisy again, either; later I came to miss her, but she was nowhere to be found.

Our Hao Bi, his shirt collar happened to be caught by the steel rods, and he tried to disentangle himself but was afraid of being dragged to his death should he lose balance on his bike. So he tried to hold on tightly to the handlebars. He was so carried by the truck at fifty miles per hour, white hair trembling in the air, while screaming his heart out for help. But the driver in front didn't hear him at all. In great noise, the truck kept moving, passed seventeen or eighteen traffic lights and headed toward a road outside the town. It never intended to use the brakes or reduce its speed, because its destination was far, far away. Exactly where Hao Bi had his life saved remained a mystery to us, as it was a detail that even he himself couldn't remember.

Monsters at Volleyball

At lunch forty of us went to play football at the pitch under Chengxi Bridge. It was a perfect square, each side with its own rusty goal. It was a weird place to play. We split into four teams as if playing four-army chess, all chasing one ball. You could shoot into any of the other three goals but whichever team let in the most goals lost. It looked like a gang fight, but it was just a bit of fun.

As I was going for the ball an elbow landed square on my nose. At first I thought it was snot dripping from my nose, but after I wiped it my hand came away smeared in blood. I stuffed a handkerchief into my nostrils and left the pitch to have a fag. I studied our dreary grey surroundings, the bridge in winter looked more tattered than my trousers, a row of withered brown dawn redwoods obscuring the river. We were far from the city and the area was bare apart from the morning fog which had yet to lift.

I sat for a while. Fancy Pants came over to borrow a cigarette. "We're like a bunch of crazies," he said.

Everyone goes a bit crazy in this weather, it makes you feel better. If you don't, you would be like the weather that blocks the sun from showing its face even at noon time.

Hog's Intestine came over. Hog's Intestine is a fatty because of irregular hormone secretion, so he weighs over a hundred kilos. He can't run. How the hell he got into the Chemical Engineering Technical School's class of '89 no one will ever f--king work out. Over a hundred kilos! A guy like him couldn't fix a water pump any more than he could defend like Rijkaard. Once, when we were playing basketball, he fell on Mangy and snapped one of his ribs.

"Give me a cig," Hog's Intestine said.

"Get lost, you never buy any," I said.

"Then give me a puff," he said.

I gave him my cigarette. He took a drag and gave it back but I didn't want it. Watching him suck on the cigarette, it struck me that his lips looked like a pair of buttocks. I looked up and wiped my nose with the handkerchief. The blood seemed to have stopped.

We were apprentices on the assembly line of a factory two kilometers west of the bridge, dropped in the middle of total wilderness. In those days the city had yet to expand beyond the old city moat. It was like it was in hibernation, everyone stayed inside the city. Every morning we crossed the city and went out to the factory, where we horsed around for the entire day. As soon as the bell went, we left alongside the worn-out workers, then went looking for somewhere else to horse around. Most people who passed this place thought it was being guarded, but Bandit said nobody watched over it, so we brought a ball.

"What's that?" Bulky Five came and stood beside me, pointing to a building in the distance.

It was lost in a brownish, unhealthy chemical fog. It looked like a glass ashtray.

"Sports centre for the town's new development area," Fancy Pants said. "They built it over a year ago, it was in the news."

"Looks like they built it a hundred years ago."

"The weather's bad today."

"Have you been there? Do they hold matches?"

"I don't like playing sports, I don't even like watching sports, so why the hell would I go there?" Fancy Pants said. "Think about it, when have we ever had a proper match over here? Apart from running around like f--king idiots, and winning that Worker's City Cup, what matches are there in this city? We've never had one. We just run around like f--king idiots."

"The sports centre's finished, maybe they'll have provincial level matches now?" Hog's Intestine made a face like a concerned citizen.

"Last year's provincial ping pong championship was held in the city stadium, I went to see it." I looked down and the blood started pouring from my nose again, so I raised my head and continued, "They played well, especially the girls. Still, they have no chance of making the national team, here in the Ping Pong Kingdom. It's like ink brush writing, it doesn't matter how much you practice, your writing's not going to be hung on the walls of the Great Hall of the People. So I'm telling you, you f--king idiot, provincial level matches aren't worth watching."

At that point Mr. Chen, one of the teachers from our school, came over. Mr. Chen is a young, bookishly pale kind of guy. His full name was Chen Guozhen and as a staff member of our school he handled political and ideological stuff, kept tabs on who's fighting who, who's smoking, and had to follow us out to this godforsaken place for our apprenticeships. Upon seeing him I threw away my cigarette. "For f--k's sake," he said, "you're playing football instead of working? You f--king idiots want a workout, huh? Go to the workshop and work your f--king muscles there. I'm confiscating the ball. Big Fly, where did you kick the ball? Go get it for me. F--king hell."

We dragged behind him, leaving Big Fly to run off into clumps of reeds by himself. As soon as we got to the factory I slipped into the medical room. It was warm in there. I waited for half an hour before the nurse arrived. She asked me what I was doing there. I told her I had a nose bleed and needed some sterilized cotton. She was very sympathetic but after searching for a long time she couldn't find any. Eventually she chucked a surgical mask at me and told me to rip it open and pull the cotton out. I wasn't actually still bleeding so I thought I might as well wear the mask as I headed back to the workshop. As I walked in I saw Cat-Face and a few of the kids from the Light Industry Academy fighting. Normally we would rush over to help whoever it was and crushed those nauseating school kids but this time none of us stood up, we just watched as they smashed Cat-Face's head. In fact, we clapped and whooped.

Just goes to show what a bunch of fickle and capricious jerks we were.

The Light Industry Academy kids were our sworn enemies. The Academy wasn't a university, but by studying one more year in school than regular tech school students, they were classified as future cadres, while we would be mere workers. They were shrimp among the cadres, but they were still cadres. We were sharks among the workers, but we were still only workers. It was that simple.

Take me for example. My scores at the junior high graduation exam were enough to get me into an Academy, but unfortunately I applied for the most prestigious Finance and Economics Academy, and they required even higher scores than the best academic middle schools. The Chemical Engineering Technical School was my second choice. If I'd known I would have applied for the Textile Academy; not only were the required scores low but lots of girls went there. Just my luck, only getting into the Chemical Engineering Technical School. Out of a whole class of forty there wasn't even one girl. We once all fell in love with a beautiful and coquettish teacher who taught us technical drawing. When she got pregnant we all cried.

Even so, I didn't want to fight with the Academy kids anymore. We would only get ourselves in trouble by fighting them, since they had the protection of the authorities. It didn't matter how the fight started it was always us technical school kids who got punished the worst. It was like in the Yuan dynasty, we were the lowest of the low, the Han Chinese, and the Academy kids were the assorted minority groups who ranked above us in the pecking order. I'd been here for two years and was about to graduate, I didn't want this extra trouble right at the last moment.

Big Fly didn't come back all afternoon so in the evening I went to find him, to tell him that his least favorite Cat-Face got a beating and had to go to hospital for stitches. But Big Fly wasn't in the mood to talk about Cat-Face. "I went to the sports centre this afternoon," he said instead.

"Fun?"

"Really fun. I'll take you tomorrow." Big Fly noticed that I wasn't too impressed. I was obviously keen to keep talking about Cat-Face's beating, so he decided to give away his big secret. "The girls practice there."

"What girls?"

"The volleyball team, provincial level," Big Fly said, counting his fingers, "there must be more than ten of them, twelve at least. All really tall, taller than me. Taller than you even."

I looked at him sympathetically. Big Fly was a short-ass, strong but short. As if to make up for his shortness, he liked tall girls, like Broody who went to the Textile Academy and towered half a head above him.

When I was small the Chinese women's volleyball teams were role models renowned for their fighting spirit. Even my strict mother allowed me to stay up until the middle of the night to watch them play. If I didn't get to see their matches I couldn't focus on my composition, and then I'd be told off by my teacher. I kind of hated them at the same time. I first went to a volleyball court around the time I had grown to one seventy-eight. The net was taller than I'd imagined, when I jumped I could only just get four fingertips above it. It was embarrassing. That was when I realized how tall volleyball girls were. I like girls half a head shorter than me. If I were with a girl taller than me by a head— well, I've never experienced it, I don't know how it would feel.

"I'll come with you tomorrow," I said to Big Fly.

The next day at lunchtime we went back to the pitch. Following Cat-Face's battering Mr. Chen was afraid we were going to try to get back at them, so that day he let us go play. But who was going to bother getting revenge for a loser like Cat-Face? The gang had completely forgotten about him and were busy kicking up dust on the pitch instead, enjoying our hard-won freedom. "The girls' volleyball team plays at the sports centre,"

I told them. After that no one wanted to keep playing, they all wanted to trek through the reeds to take a look. Big Fly wasn't pleased and swore at me.

The weather was pretty good that day, the mist was gone and the sun was out. As we walked, the dry, dead leaves of grass were floating up into the air, as if we were doing some serious damage to them. The ground was so dry it was soft, the soil was loose. It was really comfortable to walk on. If only the pitch was this comfortable.

As we approached the sports centre it towered above us like a humungous assembly workshop, with dark green walls and tea-colored glass. An assembly workshop can never be round, I thought angrily—why did I think of that? How idiotic. Winter weeds were floating all round us and nearby stood an abandoned worksite. It looked as if they'd been conducting an archaeological dig, and having finished excavating they drove in some poles and left the pit open. This place was so different from the city it was like being in another country. They said lots of foreign companies were advertising jobs out here and they paid well. A brand new sports centre symbolized new life rising from the ground.

We swaggered in but it was deadly quiet, there wasn't even anyone at the door. Our gang swaggers boldly everywhere (except maybe the police station), and everywhere we swagger we get stopped (except at the police station). It was indeed massive inside. It had high ceilings, a viewing platform surrounding a court across which someone had strung a volleyball net. There wasn't a soul inside. We were disappointed. Fancy Pants sat high on the stand and lit up a cigarette, others followed him and sat down as well. The cigarette started making its way around the group. When it got to me I stubbed it out. "You can't smoke in here."

"You f--king idiot," Bulky Five said, "there's no one here. First you bring us down here and then you don't let us smoke."

"The athletes can't breathe in any smoke, it damages their lungs. My uncle said so." They all knew about my uncle. He's a provincial level fencer.

"There's no one f--king here." Bulky Five isn't a very eloquent kid, he repeats every sentence about ten times until he gets fed up and stops.

"I can't possibly call out the volleyball girls and ask them to play for you, can I?"

"If we'd known we would've sent you ahead to check first, let you waste your own time," Bulky Five continued, "there's no one here, for f--k's sake. I don't even like volleyball. I like football."

That idiot liked nothing more than to play one-man football, with the sky as his goal. Volleyball meant nothing to him. I ignored him and went by myself to the net. I jumped up and made a volleyball spike. I was delighted to discover my elbow reached over the net. I tried again just to check and I was right. This meant that my spikes wouldn't fly out towards the spectator seats anymore.

"What are you doing, idiot?" Big Fly had sat down on the spectator platform and was shouting at me.

"I can spike the ball," I said. "Chuck me your football, I'll show you."

"Spike a football? Are you insane?" Big Fly said. "You want to give us a show?"

"You don't know shit, last term I could barely reach the net. Now I can already get my elbow above it. That means I can do a smash. I've got better at jumping, after all I haven't grown any taller these past six months."

No one cared, only Quiff came running over. Quiff was the tallest in our class at one eighty-two. He jumped up in his leather shoes and flicked his hand. "What's so great about that, I can do it too."

"But last term I couldn't reach," I said.

"Last term you got dumped by a girl from the Academy of Light Industry," Big Fly shouted from afar. "You shrunk after that, you couldn't reach anything. But it seems you've got back on your feet this year."

Just as I tried jumping up again a girl appeared at the other side of the net. She was wearing a full volleyball strip and was taller than me by about half a head. She had a volleyball tucked under her elbow, and was laughing at me. I froze.

"Last year you were jumping against the men's net, our girl's net is lower by twenty centimeters."

The court had an echo so the idiots behind me all heard and bent over laughing.

Their practice was closed to the public so we were ushered out and went sit outside the sports centre to cool down. We couldn't see through the tea-colored glass, only our reflections. Soon we were bored and out of cigarettes. Quiff needed to take a piss so he ran over to the worksite and peed into the hole. The rest of us joined in. "We should have pissed at the tea-colored glass, we can't see anything inside anyway," Haobi said once we'd finished.

"And you'd be comfortable taking that tiny dick out in front of people?" Fancy Pants asked.

Haobi was the disabled kid in our class. His hair was graying prematurely, he lisped, and he had a really small dick. If you pulled down his trousers you'd think he was a girl at first. But you only had to hear him swear to know he was a guy. He told Fancy Pants to f--k off at least twenty times. Fancy Pants didn't respond, not even with his fists, mostly because Fancy Pants hardly ever gets into fights. He always tries to maintain a strange sort of dignity, and in the rare moments he does answer back his obscenities are so fruity the other person is already wild with anger before he's even finished. He turned and said to me, "Haobi's been drinking some sort of herbal drinks these past few days, Apollo's Salts or something for the enlargement of penis. Apparently the enlargement can cause agitation."

We walked back to the factory.

The whole way Fancy Pants kept asking me about how the girl from the Light Industry Academy dumped me. He was dating someone, and it seemed his girlfriend was about to get rid of him, so he was keen to prepare himself for how it might feel. "I can't be bothered to talk about it, ask Big Fly," was my reply.

"This f--king idiot here fell for a girl at the Academy," Big Fly said. "I saw her, a rather plain-looking girl, but she had these dimples like that actress Zhong Chuhong. He stopped dead at the sight of these dimples, like when Bulky Five gets sight of a bottle of Chinese vodka. So he went to her school and asked her out. What was her name?"

"Li Xia," I said.

"Yeah, Li Xia. She was pretty good to him at first, bought him sodas. She was from a town outside the city, didn't talk like us and lived in a group dorm. Idiot over here likes girls who live in group dorms."

"Because no one is in charge of those who live in a dorm," Fancy Pants suggested. "But even if you start dating one there's no future in it. They always go back home to their small towns after graduation."

Big Fly continued. "Once she took us to see volleyball, their School has a volleyball court. We went with her to the court and watched them play. But no one realized she liked one of them, the best-looking one, what was his name?"

"Zhang Min," I said.

"Yeah, Zhang Min. F--king idiot watched for hours before he realized Li Xia had her eyes fixed on this guy. He got jealous, marched on to the court in his leather shoes and made a dig pass, Zhang Min returned it in a backward flight. This idiot jumped up to block the shot and the ball went smashing into his face. Smashed right in his face!" He laughed.

"What's funny about that?" asked Fancy Pants.

"You weren't there," Big Fly said. "I was there. I thought I was gonna go crazy from laughing. F--king idiot covered his face and lay down on the court. Everyone was pissing themselves, Li Xia was laughing so much she was nearly on the floor with him. This idiot was too embarrassed to go see her again."

"Now, that is funny," Fancy Pants said, his face still stone-serious. "No wonder he was practicing spikes today."

"Somebody hit me in the face with a ball, that's all," I said. "Big Fly, remember the time you got kicked in the balls by Li Xiao? You were both trying to get with Broody and he kicked you square in the nuts. Are they still there?"

Big Fly lunged at me and tried to kick my balls but I dodged behind Fancy Pants. Fed up, Fancy Pants shook his head and cupped his balls for protection. "Don't be so pathetic," he said. A flock of birds flapped up out of the reeds and into the air, swept over our heads and landed again in the distance. Did we scare them off, or were they just looking for a new place to hang out?

When we got to the factory entrance Mr. Chen was smoking in the reception. He pointed at us and said, "Have you f--king losers been playing football again? I told you, don't think about Cat-Face. In life, if you get a beating, you get a beating. It's bad luck, that's all. All you idiots do is fight. Don't bring me more trouble or you're all expelled."

Cat-Face had four stitches at the hospital and appeared a few days later in the workshop looking like a wounded soldier. We were screwing nuts into the lid of a large basin. The workshop supervisor had handed out twenty wrenches, one for every two students. Once we finished he collected the wrenches and discovered there were only ten left. As he was shouting abuse at us Cat-Face walked over, his face tied up in bandages. His face was big at the best of times but now it bulged like a gourd. Cat-Face grabbed one of the wrenches and started waving it around. The supervisor was frightened. "What are you doing?"

"Where are the kids from the other school? Call them in."

"The f--k it's got to do with me, you want a fight don't do it here. If you are a real man, go burn down their houses."

"F--k, I was beaten in the entrance to the workshop, and now that I want to get them back you want me to do it someplace else?"

The supervisor couldn't dissuade him. He thought his bark was bigger than his bite, and it served him right. With only nine of the wrenches—he wasn't going to ask for the one in Cat-Face's hand—he stomped out muttering curses and disappeared out of our sight.

Cat-Face called over a few of his best friends, went to the side and lit a cig. Together they discussed their plan of action. This kind of thing was common at our school; you kill me, I kill you back. It shocked no one. Me, Big Fly and Fancy Pants didn't get on with them so well so we weren't about to get involved in this sort of bullshit. Fancy Pants said Cat-Face wasn't going to do anything earthshaking, if he'd really wanted to get them back he would've gone quietly, by himself, with a kitchen knife. He wouldn't gather seven or eight of them and use wrenches. I'd never seen anyone use a wrench as a weapon, it looked too much like a propaganda poster with the slogan: "We Workers Are Powerful!"

That afternoon the three of us slipped out of the factory and back to the sports centre. This time we took a shortcut, following the dry, hard winter road. The weather had turned bad again and it looked like a snowstorm was gathering in the haze up above. Sometimes I wonder what would happen if the snow didn't fall gradually in flakes but just crashed down on this goddam world in one big clump. What a load of crap.

"I've been dumped," Fancy Pants said.

"You were only together a few days, weren't you?"

"Two months. She doesn't like me."

"Did you kiss her?" Big Fly asked.

"Once. She wouldn't let me a second time."

"Don't sweat it, it'll pass."

"I haven't been smashed in the face with a volleyball, or been kicked in the nuts, what have I got to sweat about?" Fancy Pants looked nonchalant. "Let's go watch the girls' volleyball team, talking to you guys about this stuff is a complete waste of time. You guys know nothing."

But the girls had already left. We had walked for half an hour for nothing. The sports centre was empty, not even the net remained. We sat down on the viewing platform and caught our breath.

"Probably the training's over," Big Fly said.

"What about that tall girl from last time? I've never seen such a tall girl. Big Fly, you're into tall girls right? She was taller than me!" I said.

"She was too tall," Big Fly muttered, depressed. "She must have been taller than me by more than a full f--king head."

I shut my eyes to think for a second, but I couldn't bring to mind what she looked like. She was indeed tall enough and I kind of admired a girl I had literally to look up to, just the way I admire writers, policemen, engineers. That's a f--king irritating feeling. I even admired that Zhang Min who'd thrown a ball in my face, he was about the same height as me but his calves were long and so full of spring. He can jump up real high to spike the ball. I can't.

An old guy walked in and shooed us out. We went to see if there were any more wild birds in the grass so it took us an hour to get back to the factory. When we got back I saw a crowd of people standing by the door to the washrooms. They'd run over after the last bell as if they'd been rushing for the winter sales. I'd just seen so many birds take flight, and they'd been so calm, far more composed than any human. Only later did I realize those people wanted to wash and get back to their homes before the snow came. But the snow didn't come. Cloudy days make people paranoid.

Mr. Chen called us to the factory canteen for a meeting. It was midmorning and the place was empty. In a moment of candor Mr. Chen said, "If you're planning on getting your own back you're going to get expelled. Anyone who gets into a fight will be expelled. Bloody hell, you're just trying to make it hard for me to live my life on my salary, is that it?"

Cat-Face spoke up, "Kids of the other school beat me up pretty badly and not one of them got expelled."

"How do I know what's going on at the other school?" Mr. Chen said. "I work at the Chemical Engineering Technical School, I have no right to expel students of the other school. But I can expel you lot."

"If you want reconciliation tell them they can buy me dinner. They can kowtow before me and serve me tea. Else this isn't over."

"F--king hell," Mr. Chen said, "you guys think you're a bunch of gangsters? If it weren't for me protecting you, you'd have been expelled at least twenty times this term alone. Once you're expelled you can get anyone you like to kowtow before you. You can bring the whole mafia in here and make me kowtow. But till then, no. F--k."

Then Mr. Chen left. I felt a bit sad after hearing what he had to say because I've seen Cat-Face be made to kowtow before and it's not like you just kowtow and everything's resolved. He had his face stamped on. They spat on the ground and made him lick it clean. It's no fun, no fun at all.

"I want to get someone to snap their foot tendons." And Cat-Face left too.

The next day Mr. Chen brought us back to the canteen. "Shit, things are pretty f--king bad. Those guys from the other school are too scared to come to the factory for their apprenticeship. They went to speak to their headmaster, who went to speak to our headmaster, who came to speak to me. If any of you dare do a thing I'm done for. F--k it, whatever. You die how you want to die. If you've got it in you to go pick a fight at the other school I might as well go along and get killed too."

Cat-Face looked depressed. It was easy to retaliate within the factory walls, but going to the other school would be effectively declaring war. We'd need ten times more people than them and ten times the weaponry. A wrench wouldn't cut it. For one thing, Cat-Face would never be able to find enough people and we all knew that even if he could it'd cost him serious money. Some of them wouldn't even fight, they'd only be there for the free food and drink. But there's no way you could go over there with a squadron of three, you'd need backup in the form of a whole load of idiots to make it look like a proper battle: the front line force, the guard patrol, hell even the song and dance troupe and the kitchen staff.

Me, Big Fly and Fancy Pants yawned and walked off. The night before we'd played mahjong till morning, we were tired, we couldn't be bothered with work let alone getting involved in this stuff. In our group only Big Ass was itching to have a go. He was a sicko, he only had to see a fight to want to get involved. Sometimes, when he saw women having arguments with the vegetable sellers in the market, he would join in the fray with his fists. He had raging hormones. "Big Ass, you shouldn't be living in China," Fancy Pants said, "you should go to Africa and hunt." We decided to go find somewhere to sleep.

Come lunchtime we were kicked awake. We looked up. It was Mr. Chen. We had no idea what he was doing. "F--king sleeping, eh? The headmaster's coming, do me a favor and get yourselves over."

I rubbed my eyes. What was this about? The headmaster, rode a bike all the way down to this far-flung place? Not likely. Then I realized it was because of Cat-Face, he said he wanted to snap their foot tendons, didn't he? We close friends never believed him when he said shit like that, the idiot didn't even know where the tendons were on his own foot. But to normal people it would sound scary, like a country threatening to drop an atom bomb.

We lined up and waited for the headmaster. He was short and fat, like Napoleon, and whenever he made inspections he put on a Napoleonic air. Accompanied by Mr. Chen, he started by examining our spiritual outlook. Apart from the three of us who'd just woken up, the rest were alright. Once that was over he put his hands on waist and began pontificating on world affairs, the latest news stories and political trends. After that he looked at Cat-Face's injuries, indicated that a few knocks were nothing and comforted comrade Cat-Face with some warm words. Trying to get revenge was not the wisest course of action, we must attempt instead to turn our enemies into our friends, and be strong as men. His educator's demeanor was in full show. He was patient and methodical in his guidance. Mr. Chen was standing behind him, nodding, glancing now and then at Cat-Face's injured mug. Cat-Face had never before been on the receiving end of comforting words like this, and he looked like a kitten closing his eyes with pleasure at being stroked. Then suddenly he started crying. We all breathed a sigh of relief and thought about how magnificent the headmaster was; he'd exposed Cat-Face as a crazy with such effortless ease.

"In order to strengthen relations between the various light industry educational institutions, including the Academy, the Technical School and the Vocational School, we are going to hold a sporting competition. Sport for friendship. Volleyball, that's a good sport, I am willing to approve a volleyball competition. What do you think?"

We nodded unenthusiastically. What else were we going to do?

The headmaster turned to Mr. Chen and said, "You organize it. This group of boys is the core of my school, let them take the court." He patted Cat-Face's shoulder and said, "You take part too. Use your fists on the ball, not other people." Cat-Face was sobbing so hard he was nearly out of breath.

The school of Chemical Engineering's class of '89 was made up entirely of boys, not a single girl among us. Some people call this kind of group a "monk's class," or a "hooligan class." When they play balls, all that's needed is the slightest contact, flesh on flesh, and there'll be a fight. I once watched Bulky Five playing football. He limped his way up the pitch, dribbling the ball and calling, "I'll kill whoever dares take the ball off me!" And so he managed to dribble the ball right into the opponent's goal. We suggested he balanced the ball on his nose like a seal instead, since no one dared tackle him anyway. There wasn't a sporting bone among us. Tackling in football gets you into a fight, but with volleyball there's a net in the way, just like in ping pong.

If you can't get the ball you just smack yourself in the face. Our headmaster's a genius if you ask me, he knew we'd fight over a game of chess but wouldn't run around a volleyball net to beat up the other guys. That would be just too low, even for us.

If the Light Industry Academy had one strength, it was volleyball. They had an after-school club and Zhang Min could deliver a backward flight beautifully. Our strength wasn't football, or Chinese kickboxing, but just acting like a bunch of f--king idiots until everyone was disappointed. I spent the whole night thinking about it, Cat-Face had done well out of it alright, he'd managed to get us to take part in a high-level sports match without a hope in hell of winning. I dreamed that I was wandering between the factory and the sports centre in the new development area, wild birds flying up around me, the snow falling in large, swirling flakes. I was wearing shorts and was freezing. I kept fighting off balls that were flying at me. It was f--king exhausting. Then instead of balls it was wrenches and I woke up.

On a winter afternoon not longer after that, we got on our bikes and rode to the Light Industry Academy. Mr. Chen took us. The headmaster was going to come but he had to go to a meeting. Walking into the School felt strangely familiar. Yeah, I'd been out with a girl who went here, I'd been here loads of times. I almost thought of going to her dorm. The thought was quite painful, my face smarting from the memory of getting smashed by a volleyball.

They were already on the court waiting for us. There were lots of girls in that school, that made it the object of my envy, and they'd formed a brightly colored cheerleading team, clapping and cheering as we entered. The court was a square slab of concrete, perfectly flat and clean with white, straight lines painted on it. The net was already strung across. The forty of us cringed. Our team was a ragtag bunch, made up of short, tall, fat and scrawny guys, each one different. Mr. Chen whispered, "Focus guys, I don't f--king want to be here either, the headmaster sent me. Play well and I'll give you a day off." We nodded. Mr. Chen looked at all of us.

"Who's up?" We looked at each other in dismay. "You haven't even talked it over? What the hell are you doing here then?"

"Waiting for you to pick the team."

"How the f--k do I know which one of you plays volleyball? Who doesn't play? Choose yourselves. Quick."

The other team appeared and the first one I saw was Zhang Min. He was wearing an official volleyball strip in this cold weather as if the freezing temperature could do nothing to knock the power out of him. He started jumping up and down to show off his physique. He was the king of jumping. In actual fact he wasn't that good-looking, just kind of chiseled with a flouncy haircut. It was enough to make him the focus of the court. Of course all the girls started shouting, "Go Zhang Min!" He ran a lap around the court smiling. They were all flouncy, the whole team, and although they weren't brave enough to wear shorts like him, they were all wearing track pants with two stripes down them and trainers. Those two strong, beautiful legs were Zhang Min's monopoly, and his alone.

I looked over at our team. Half of us were wearing leather shoes, half knitted cotton trousers, all of us woolen jumpers. Even the most imposing of us, Big Ass, was wearing a leather jacket. "F--king hell, what are you doing here? Playing ball or dressed for a date?" I couldn't stop myself.

"We look like a bunch of stupid ass." Fancy Pants asked, "Who's the one in shorts?"

"Zhang Min, the one who spiked the ball in Lu Xiaolu's face," Big Fly said.

"F--king idiot," Fancy Pants said, "if we'd worn shorts, he'd have had to play with his dick out in order to show off."

We spread out and did some warm-ups while picking a provisional team. A girl came over for fun, and asked, "Why didn't you bring any cheerleaders?"

"We're our own cheerleaders," I said. "We don't have any girls at our school, would you be interested in watching a cheerleader group made up by a bunch of losers?"

"Yeah," she laughed.

"Don't care, not going to show you."

We started choosing the team. It was like deciding who was going to pay the bill, no one was allowed to back down. I was selected first and I didn't want to play but I had no choice. I ran a lap around the court to the sound of some friendly clapping; they had forgotten that I was the one who got a volleyball in the face. I jumped up to touch the net and my heart sank, they'd strung it at men's regulation height, I could only get four fingers above it. It wasn't that I thought that all of the guys on the other side could jump higher than me, but that Zhang Min certainly could.

"Short legs! Long torso!" The girls were laughing at me.

I didn't care. I don't get angry with girls. They were laughing at me because they compared me to Zhang Min, and if Zhang Min wasn't playing they'd like me. If we were fighting with words rather than a volleyball they'd want to marry me. That's what I wanted to believe.

The second one up was Cat-Face, he had to be on the team. He stuffed his hands in his pockets. His head was still wrapped in a bandage and he skulked onto the court, spitting a wad of phlegm. This isn't a f--king football pitch, I thought, who said you could spit wherever you want? Cat-Face couldn't find the three guys who'd beat him up, so he shrugged and stood where he was, pulled his hands out of his pockets and cracked his fingers forcefully as if he was about to start a fight. The crowd started clapping again.

The third one picked was Big Ass. He was a bit short but he'd make an okay feeder, despite the fact that normally he couldn't catch a cigarette so you couldn't exactly expect him to be any good at catching a volleyball. Quiff was forth to be picked, he was the romantic type and had been chatting with the girls nonstop, even as he walked on the court. Bulky Five was fifth, and he went straight to kick Quiff in the butt to get him to focus. It was important to him to win. As for the sixth we had no one, no one would agree to play. After a lengthy discussion they kicked Fancy Pants into the court. "I hate playing balls," Fancy Pants said loudly, "I'll go on, but don't expect me to move a muscle." The crowd shushed.

The referee was a PE teacher from the School. He grabbed a bench and stood by the net. First came the rules: best of five, change service after fifteen points. No one understood the stuff about rotating positions. "Whatever, it doesn't matter," Zhang Min said loudly. "They don't understand. Let's hurry up and play, I'm freezing." I nodded and replied, "We don't understand, that's right, and if we delay any longer those legs will turn into Eskimo Pie." The referee relented.

At that moment I caught sight of Li Xia.

She was a good-looking girl, it wasn't just her dimples that attracted me. There was a lot I liked about her, but, like boredom, I just couldn't pinpoint the reasons behind it. She was standing at the edge of the court looking at me the whole time. It was cold and she was clutching a pink water bottle, nodding at me with a smile on her face. I couldn't help myself, I ran over to her. "You haven't been to see me in ages," she said. I looked at her dimples, first the left then the right. Her complexion wasn't too good. "I've come to play volleyball," I said.

"Play your best, I'll be cheering for you," she said.

She was so soft and gentle, and gentle girls like her loved to laugh, it was natural for her to laugh at seeing me making a fool of myself. I was no longer angry with her. With a pair of dimples like that, it would be a shame if she didn't laugh. I thought of the time she complained about how boring school life was, every day from the dorm to the classroom and back again. She hardly ever got to watch TV, she could only read, and she didn't enjoy that much. I wasn't put on this earth to be laughed at, I thought, but I could be laughed at as long as I was willing.

My neck tensed. Mr. Chen was pulling me back onto the court.

"I'll come see you after the match," I said to Li Xia.

I don't know why she wrinkled her brows. She found a bench, sat down and nestled her hot water bottle underneath her clothes and against her lower belly. She was watching me, not Zhang Min and his beautiful legs.

"Is that the girl you like?" Fancy Pants asked.

"Yeah."

"She's got period cramps," Fancy Pants said. "I can tell by just looking at her. Period cramps. Bad things, hurts like crazy."

"What should I do?"

"My girlfriend got cramps. We were only together for two months so I only saw it twice. She said she had to lie flat and use a hot water bottle. That and drink molasses."

I ran over to her and said, "Why don't you go back to your dorm?"

"I'm fine. I came to watch you."

"F--king hell Lu Xiaolu, what's going on?" Mr. Chen said. I ran back onto the court. As soon as the referee blew the whistle the ball came flying over and Bulky Five made a tiger fist and punched the ball right into Cat-Face's butt. Everyone started laughing. "F--k, no laughing allowed," Bulky Five said, "don't anybody get in my way!"

I turned to look at Li Xia. There was a gentle, pained look on her face. Then she laughed. Because it really was funny. We idiots deserved to be laughed at. I was happy for her to laugh at me just as she was happy to come see me when she had period cramps. A fair swap I'd say. I couldn't be bothered to play, and by the time we were nil-five down I couldn't take it anymore. I couldn't hear the laughter, Zhang Min was so cold he was shivering, and he never got the chance to jump up to do a backward flight or a spike. He should have missed me by now. At least I could still f--king whack the ball, I just didn't want to. At one point the ball went flying towards Li Xia—that was the only time I bothered to reach out and hit it. Then I looked across and saw Fancy Pants reluctantly lifted his foot and placed it on the ball to stop it rolling around. I raised my hand to leave the game.

"I'm hurt," I said.

"Where?" Mr. Chen asked.

"He's got period cramps," Fancy Pants answered for me.

I ignored Mr. Chen's abuse. The whole thing was too f--king funny. Anyway, I'd done my bit, just like my dad and the socialist education movement, or my uncle with factional fightings during the Cultural Revolution, or when my uncle on my mother's side helped bring down the Gang of Four. As long as you take part, history will leave its mark on your rear end. And Mr. Chen had definitely left his mark on mine. When I left the court, I saw the remaining thirty-four bastards sitting on the ground laughing. Fancy Pants left the court at the same time. "Those were the ten most f--king boring minutes of my life," he said. He walked off to the bike sheds in the distance. After that the bastards pushed graying Hao Bi and the fatso Hog's Intestine into the centre of the court. Everyone was wetting themselves with laughter.

I didn't want to watch any more, so I ran over to Li Xia. "It's too cold, I'll take you back to your dorm."

"Okay," she said, "I can't take much more."

She stood up but I didn't dare touch her. She walked really slowly and at first I walked close by her. We left the court, leaving the mess behind us. I heard Big Fly shout, "F--k, I don't want to play!" Big Fly was kicked onto the court. The team now consisted of a bandaged Cat-Face with a murderous look on his face, white-haired, frail Hao Bi, dumb ass Hog's Intestine, the grandstanding Quiff, crazy Bulky Five, a furious Big Ass who didn't want to be taken out, and short-ass Big Fly who didn't want to play the game. Seven in total. All facing Zhang Min's beautiful legs. Distressed, Big Fly said, "I don't f--king want to play volleyball."

Li Xia and I now walked side by side. "I haven't been to see you in ages. Time really flies."

"Yeah, I will graduate next term. I'm going to work in the city's new development area. I'm really happy."

"Me too. The new development area has a big stadium, for volleyball and other sports."

My heart fluttered. Then it did it again. But I didn't look back. I just walked away with her.

The Book Thief

Nobody would have expected a bookshop to open next to a technical school, because we tech school students just didn't read books! At that time—I'm talking about the year 1990—we were obsessed with videos, video games, mahjong, and imported cigarettes. But no one read books. No one read martial arts novels either. Anyone who said he liked Gu Long, Jin Yong (most renowned martial arts novelists), or Li Xunhuan, Yang Guo (best known martial art heroes) was a f--king idiot living in a fantasy world of pressure points, qi, and other stuff like that. If you wanted to go out and got in fights, you only needed to know two things: first, don't get your head cracked open, and second, clear out when you hear the cops. I'm telling you, in 1990, only artsy types were interested in martial arts novels.

No one would have thought that a girl would open a bookshop right across from our Chemical Engineering School.

The school was in a rural-urban transition zone. One side was the city, with several new housing developments and a huge population. On the other side were a wharf, a huge warehouse area, and a desolate highway. As it happened, the school sat right on this dividing line, so if we needed some modern entertainment, we could go into the city. If we wanted to cut loose, all we had to do was go out of the city. We could fight and pick up chicks inside or outside the city.

So, when we saw the bookshop open, we found it pretty strange. Bookshops mostly exist next to secondary schools, they sell stationery and other supplies essential for students. As for us, the whole school only had 200 students, and 90% were male. Most of us just wanted to get the hell out of there. I didn't even have a satchel. Every day as I rode my bike to school, I would hang my father's black leather briefcase on my handlebars. It was really thin, with three zippered sides. Stuck inside were my pencil and ballpoint pen. My cigarettes and lighter were hidden away in a separate pouch. There wasn't any room for books.

I remember it was in the afternoon of the second day the store opened when Quiff and I passed by and saw a girl sat at the store entrance gently waving a feather duster. Quiff suddenly pulled up short, like he was under a spell.

"Since when was there a bookstore here?"

"It opened yesterday," I said. "You skipped class yesterday, that's why you're just seeing it now."

The girl said, "Come on over and check out some books!"

Quiff said, "You should say: 'Come on over and *buy* some books.' If we just read the books, we'll ruin them."

"I'm renting books." She gathered up her feather duster, giving Quiff a coy smile. By the time he was 17, this son of a bitch was pretty good-looking; in fact, he had skipped school the day before to go get his hair coiffed. Lots of girls gave him coy smiles. But I think it was her smile that had his soul stolen from him.

"Maybe I'll come on over and check you out," Quiff said.

Then we headed back to school. I said to Quiff, "There's no use in you going to see her. That bookstore will close down soon and she'll be gone with it."

Quiff was optimistic, "Maybe it won't close down just yet. Maybe I'll get expelled before then. You never know what'll happen."

Thus this bookshop, or should I say book rental, sprang up opposite the technical school. It was on the other side of a lousy little street with no pedestrian walk, no trees and no people, even the power line poles clung to the houses and walls. No one wanted to walk on the street. Sometimes we would stand at the school gate and look at the bookstore. It was dark in there, with the vague visage of the girl sitting in the corner. I went there once. Half the books were run-down martial arts books and mushy romance novels, and the other half were foreign and revolutionary novels. They were arranged according to genre on the shelves. Neither half interested me. When the weather was good, she would go out and sit in the sun. I could say for sure that her shop had no business. She just chose the wrong place.

Perhaps she was too lonely, she felt that Quiff could relieve her boredom from the very beginning. And he didn't disappoint. On many afternoons, he would sit on a little stool in her shop. This struck us as very strange. We had strolled over to take a look. Big Fly said he didn't think the girl was very pretty, though she had a refined air about her. The others didn't know the meaning of "refined." I said, "I think she's gray. When I look at her, I feel like I've gone colorblind."

Big Fly said, "No one understands what the hell you're talking about."

That year Quiff had fallen in love with all kinds of girls. By his count, there were about fifteen, including that girl from the grade above, Coco, Li Xia from the Academy of Light Industry, the street girl Noisy, and a bunch of other nameless girls, all to no avail. His only success came with our school librarian, Lu Lily. But Lily wasn't very good-looking. And she was five years older than Quiff. Every time Lily was mentioned, Quiff would lower his head, like a plane coming in for a landing.

"I think Lu Lily suits you better," Big Fly said.

"Come on, we're supposed to be friends. Give me a break," Quiff said. "I don't like older girls, you like that kind of girl."

"Have you f--ked that girl from the bookstore?"

"No."

"Are you planning to? You f--king skulk around her place all day."

"It's not as simple as you think." Quiff swatted at Big Fly. "It's complicated. But for you it's simple. When you are straddled by older women all you have to do is to lie there and let them do all the work."

"That's not true. Sometimes we need to change positions." Big Fly shamelessly came up behind Quiff, put his hands on his waist, and made humping motions.

Quiff nearly jumped out of his skin.

After Quiff left, Big Fly told me, "Quiff hasn't figured out what he wants. Actually, he does want to sleep with that girl from the bookstore, but he doesn't have any experience. He doesn't know that what he wants is just that simple." In addition, Big Fly said Quiff was hiding something: that girl from the bookstore and Lily were both five years older than him. He still thought no one else knew.

"I think she's old," I said, "like a witch."

One day, on the side of the warehouse, we were looking for smokes in Quiff's bag and we turned up Part Two of *Les Miserables*. The author was some French guy, Hugo. The guys who didn't know Quiff laughed at him, saying that he had turned into a cultured man, reading such a thick book, and Part Two at that, that means that he had finished Part One! Actually, we all knew the story of *Les Miserables*. There was a dubbed version of the movie. But who would have the patience to go and read the whole thing? Embarrassed, Quiff moved about and tried to snatch the book back, but it was tossed back and forth by the group until it finally came in the direction of Fancy Pants. Fancy Pants said, "He's just reading a book, there's nothing wrong with that. You guys have no life." He didn't reach out to catch the book, and it fell right into the river.

"F--k you!"

Fancy Pants just said, "This guy is possessed!"

A few days later, Quiff tried to steal a book from Xinhua Bookstore and was caught by a clerk. This wasn't such a serious matter. Xinhua Bookstore had just started using open shelves and book thieves were caught almost daily. But they did threaten to take the thief down to the police station. The bookstore called the school right off and the teacher who came down had only recently been transferred from a factory job. As soon as he got down to the bookstore, he socked Quiff. The clerk was shocked. Then the teacher pointed at Quiff and asked, "How many books did you steal?"

The clerk looked at the table and said, "*Les Misérables*. Part Two."

The teacher socked Quiff again and asked the clerk, "Enough?"

The bookstore clerk said, "That's enough and don't hit him again, just bring him back for a good talk. It might not be appropriate for a teacher of the people to hit student like that." The teacher replied, "You don't know shit. If I don't discipline him here and now, he'll get expelled for sure." The bookstore clerk said wryly, "I'd heard that your school was highly disciplined. I see your reputation is well-deserved." By that time, Quiff was bleeding from both nostrils. He looked terrible.

The next day Lu Lily stopped him, "Why did you go to the bookstore and steal *Les Misérables*? Our library has a copy, too."

The library at our technical school was right next to the dining hall. You had to turn down a small alley to find the entrance. That is to say, in the course of your normal activities, you wouldn't even know it existed. The alley wasn't even paved. Some bricks served as stepping stones when it rained, though even when it didn't rain, Lily was still in the habit of skipping over the bricks to get to the door.

Not that many people went in there to begin with. The place was narrow and really out-of-the-way. Most of the books were chemical engineering reference books, which didn't have anything to do with us, and extracurricular reading, like novels and books of essays, all of them out of date and emanating mold, no one had consulted them either. Even though she was one of the few unmarried women at the school, Lu Lily was never in our good graces. Her biggest fault was her disappointing looks. The biggest problem with her looks was her buckteeth. The movies called these Bugs Bunny teeth. Around here we call them bottle openers or beaver teeth. Her work helped her hide her shortcoming somewhat. Behind a tall table in the library she would expose only the top half of her face, from her nose up. Just her arched eyebrows, double-fold eyelids, and, right on the bridge of her nose, a mole. Unfortunately, she always ended up bumping into people at the dining hall instead, where her buckteeth were evident at a glance.

We weren't lying when we said she was his girlfriend. Here's the way it was: one day, a bunch of us were assigned to go to the library to help clean up after we finished studying. We figured it was just dusting and wiping the windows. We had no idea she would make us take all the books off the shelf and clean all the bookshelves. By the time we were half done, we became allergic and started sneezing one after another. At that point, Lily took the only face mask out of a drawer and gave it to Quiff. He was very pleased with himself at first. He put on the mask, winking at us. But after Big Fly said the mask was Lily's to conceal her buckteeth, Quiff torn it away in disgust.

We didn't know why Lily liked Quiff. It seemed that she had had a particularly good impression of him from the very beginning. It was true that he was very handsome. But he was also a son of a bitch. Perhaps she had it backwards and thought, "Even though he's a son of a bitch, he's a very handsome son of a bitch." Sometimes Lily would meddle in his affairs, she was quite strict with him when she learned about his book stealing, for example.

Quiff rolled his eyes and said, "You don't need to stick your nose in this."

Lily was very angry. When she saw us laughing off to the side, she didn't say anything more, she just bared those buckteeth and walked off. That's when I remembered something. I asked them, "One day I saw Lily practicing her calligraphy. On a newspaper she wrote, *xin yuan di zi pian.* (a famous quote of the poet Tao Yuanming, 'peace and quiet inside one's mind') What does that mean?"

Big Fly said, "It means a woman who doesn't like to social,

she sits in a corner, and no one likes to social with her."

"It's not necessarily a woman."

"Mostly women," Big Fly said with assurance.

Afterward, we saw Quiff in the bookstore. We thought he would soon become someone who sat in a corner. He had withdrawn to a dark corner by himself, distractedly thumbing through a book from the girl's bookstore. Sometimes he wouldn't even do that, he would just stare at the girl, cheeks in hands. God, this was nothing like our friend. He had become the silent type. And the bookstore girl, sometimes she would wave that feather duster, and sometimes she would just sit quietly by Quiff, both of them staring off into space.

Big Fly pursued the matter further with Quiff, "When are you finally going to just f--k her?"

"I don't know. She's a very old-fashioned girl," Quiff said.

"You're f--king old-fashioned! If you don't sleep with her, you'd better be careful that Lu Lily would sleep with you."

"Don't talk shit," Quiff said. "Lily and I are not what you think."

Perhaps he was right. Lu Lily was actually dating someone for a while. Her boyfriend was a middle-aged teacher at our school. Balding and divorced, he was an eccentric fellow. They went everywhere together. In the dining hall they sat side by side or face to face. They ate the same food, laughed at the same jokes, even nodded at the same time. Bucktoothed and balding, it was as if they were made for each other. As if these two defects themselves had their own independent awareness and the two living, breathing people didn't exist.

Unfortunately, good things never last forever. After about two months, Quiff said that Lu Lily had been dumped. The balding teacher finally got tired of those buckteeth and said goodbye. Quiff warned us that Lily's mood had been terrible lately. Under no circumstances should we go to the library and provoke her.

"Only you like to go places that have so many books!" we sneered at him.

Quiff on the other hand was about to succeed. He had tasted the flavor of love. One day he provoked two older students, who chased him into the school trying to beat him up. Not seeing any friends around, he frantically ran out the school gate and, like a wisp of smoke, slipped into the bookstore. And that got his two assailants even angrier, they went after him with wooden sticks. The bookstore girl extended her two arms and blocked their way. "You won't act like that in here!" she said.

This held them up for a while, enough time for us to get to the scene. There was some shoving and shoving back. A shouting match lasted for about half an hour in front of the bookstore, but no one had so much as thrown a punch. After that, a teacher came. The brutal one who had knocked Quiff around. We acted like nothing had happened and scattered.

Quiff said that the girl was the bravest he had ever met. He was really moved. He felt that in this dawdling life he needed a companion like her, a place where he could take shelter, a kind of tough-but-tender fierceness. Finally, he revealed his love for her one day.

"She didn't say a word, she just smiled at me," Quiff said, distressed. "Then she said that business here wasn't very good and she would need to move."

"You could go with her and become a manager of the book-renting store," Big Fly said.

A few days later, Quiff was caught again at Xinhua Bookstore. This time he stole a book called *Resurrection*. Again that same teacher went down to collar him. He was going to knock him around again, but when he got to the store, he learned that Quiff had already been knocked around by a male employee of the bookstore. He didn't say anything, just took Quiff back to school. On the road, the teacher asked him, "So how many masterpieces have you stolen in all?"

"Thirty to fifty."

"If you're that good, why don't you go rob banks? In fact, you know what? Go rob a bank. That way I won't have to worry about you."

And that was how, at noon time the next day, we got stopped by Lu Lily on the sports field. She said, "Where is Li Junyao?" That was Quiff's real name. We said we didn't know. He was probably across the street again. Lily said angrily, "Why is he stealing books again? Why? Why?" When she was angry, she would bare all her buckteeth. It was frightening!

Big Fly said, "This we can't tell you."

Fancy Pants said, "If we tell you, you'll go crazy."

I said, "Actually, you should have known already."

Lily pounced on Big Fly, grabbing his head like someone clutching a watermelon before they take a bite, and screamed, "Tell me! You don't want to see him get expelled from school, do you? If I hadn't begged them, he would have been expelled already!"

We looked at each other in dismay. She was right. If we let him keep stealing books this way, sooner or later his luck would run out and he would get expelled, or worse, sent off for reeducation. And we would have included in our circle an idiot book thief who was later sent off for reeducation, something that strains credulity. So, Big Fly spilled everything, "Quiff is in love with the girl who opened the bookshop across the street. He's been stealing books from the bookstore to give her fresh stock … Poor thing, he doesn't even know what he's doing. He loves her."

Not surprisingly, Lu Lily went nuts. She changed from the girl who wrote "peace and quiet inside one's mind" into a monster. We figured it was on account of jealousy. She grabbed Big Fly and stormed right out the door of the school. We automatically followed her to the bookshop. Quiff was indeed inside. The sound of so many people approaching noisily must have caused a racket. He popped out the door all of a sudden.

Lu Lily pointed at the girl and said, "He's been stealing books from the bookstore for you. Did you know that?"

The girl was quite calm at first. She didn't know what had happened. Her delicate features hardened and she fixed Quiff with an astonished gaze. Amid Lily's noise, I heard her ask in a soft voice, "How could you be a thief?"

Lily said, "It was all for you. He stole dozens of books from the store. He's been caught twice. Don't pretend you don't know, I know he did it at your instruction."

"No. I don't know anything about this. He brought some books here. He said they were from his house and that he had read them all and didn't want them anymore."

Lily said, "The stolen books were all new. Who would give you new books? Look in your shop. Which books are new? Other than the ones that were stolen."

Quiff pulled at Lily and said, "Let's not talk about this."

The girl said to Quiff, "I understand now. I dislike people who steal books. I'm giving all the books back to you."

He looked regretful. "Well, let me explain."

The girl looked at him, and for a moment, it seemed as if she would forgive him. He was such a handsome guy, and his face was all regret. He just kept shaking his head, paying no attention to Lily, he really did seem worthy of forgiveness. The girl walked over and pulled Quiff, saying, "Let's go in the shop and talk." At this point, our frantic Lily gave the girl a push, pushing her all the way into the shop.

"You turned him into a thief!"

Then we all laughed and heckled Quiff, saying, "Hey Quiff, it's never pleasant to deal with two women at the same time, is it? You're finished. You'd better go ahead and give Lily a clear explanation. Otherwise, she's gonna tear this place down today!"

Lily looked at us, astonished. Suddenly understanding, she raised her palm, and slapped Quiff. When she finished, she cocked her hips, grabbed his ear and said, "Now, tell these bastards and this little bookshop liar who I am."

"She's my cousin—" Quiff cried out.

At that we saw the girl turn and walk into the shop. None of us got a good look at her facial expression. For a split second, she was colorful; but, after she went back in her shop, she regained her gray. In that kind of gray, it's hard to read a person's expression. After a while, those new books, the stolen ones, the ones that no one read, came flying out the bookshop one by one like birds fighting over scraps. Finally, she slammed the door with a thump.

After that Quiff never set foot in a bookstore again. Not the small bookshop across from the school, not Xinhua, nor any other bookstore for that matter. And Lu Lily. Now we knew, Bucktooth Cousin was not to be trifled with. She stayed in a corner of the school like some sort of fierce, hidden animal. If she were to appear, there would be one heck of a show.

Six months later, a theft was investigated at the Chemical Engineering Library. By that time, the bookshop across from the school was already closed, moved to some other place. Nobody knew the whereabouts of the girl. Nobody knew her. And there was something curious about the case: on Sunday night, the thief came in over the wall and opened the door of the library with a key, removing about 300 books. An analysis of the tracks showed that the books were packed separately and thrown over the wall, after which the thief locked the door and went back out over the wall. People reckoned you'd need at least two people to pull it off, and you'd need a flatbed trike; otherwise, you wouldn't be able to move so many books. The vile thieves even ate an orange in the library and left the peel on the table! The guard at the school's gate didn't hear a sound. It was a winter night and he was dead asleep. Even if there had been a noise, he wouldn't have been willing to go out and investigate anyway. He couldn't have been sure they wouldn't have done away with him.

Monday morning, Lu Lily opened the door, went in and was scared silly by what she saw. She then turned and ran for the police. She stumbled on the pathway bricks and fell, striking her teeth on the edge of a brick and knocking out half those buckteeth.

Some people suspected that Quiff had done it, but we can confirm that he was playing mahjong with us all night. The only puzzling thing was, he was losing a lot of money, but the whole time he was smiling, smiling, smiling.

Knifed Buttocks

Every time I remember the days when I was seventeen, aside from my bastard buddies Big Fly, Fancy Pants and Quiff, and aside from those girls, the person who never fails to show up is Bulky Five. And the reason I remember him is not because of our friendship, nor because he owed me money; I remember him because he was such a fool. I have encountered my share of stupid people in life, but adding them all up, drying them in the sun and then squeezing them into juice, the level of concentrated stupidity would still be less than the stupidity of Bulky Five.

He had always thought his nickname was "Scar Five," and when dating girls he always reminded us ahead of time that he should be called by his nickname. His real name was too rustic; I didn't even want to utter the words, or the girls would laugh their heads off. He liked his nickname, but he didn't know that "Bulky Five," which shared almost the same pronunciation of the three Chinese characters of Scar Five (Daoba Wu), was also a term in the game of Go (*weiqi* in Chinese) that described a bad move that would doom the piece in the game.

At first, he had only one scar on the back of his hand. He liked his scar as much as Coco liked her coral bracelet. He bragged about how he got this souvenir in eighth grade in a brawl. His opponent was an adult-aged ruffian. He didn't win the fight, but he managed to break the older guy's nose. The ruffian then took out a pocketknife, thrusting it at his carotid artery. He stopped the knife with his bare hand; if he hadn't succeeded in stopping it he would have died, as blood from his artery shot up to the rooftops, he claimed.

We all got scared every time he talked about this knife wound. We were afraid of being knifed. On the outside we might look like a bunch of reckless and invulnerable tech school students with kung fu, but that image existed merely in speculation and in fanciful thinking. We were ordinary boys; we tried to get our abs in shape to impress girls, and not for knives.

However, Bulky Five was different—he truly was not afraid. He said he was a bloodthirsty kind of guy who loved to have scars on his body. Once in a brawl with Big Fly right in the classroom, while Big Fly had already jumped on the windowsill and was about to crawl to the ceiling like a lizard to escape, Bulky Five broke the window with his bare fist. Raising his bloody fist, Bulky Five licked his own blood and swore, "Big Fly, you are a dead man!"

Big Fly admitted total defeat and screamed, "Get this crazy guy out!"

Bulky Five came in last in the 800-meter run in our first-semester gym class. There were forty boys in my class; even the weaklings like Hao Bi and Mangy were ahead of him. Fortunately there were no girls around, or his performance would have looked even more pitiful. We later learned that he had flat feet, plus his legs were short, we laughed at it for a long while. How could a bloodthirsty guy be a damn cripple! Although he often showed off his scarred hand in front of girls in senior classes, just to demonstrate that he was a guy upon whom girls could rely, his short legs turned out to be a dead giveaway. Who would like a short-legged killer?

Coco, our most beloved senior girl, belonged to another small group, and she didn't hang out with us often. This was totally understandable, since boys of the senior class befriended her when she first entered the Tech School, and when those boys graduated she started hanging out with the boys of her class; she should have had nothing to do with us, but we happened to be a class with no girls and only forty boys. During class breaks, the boys' room would be so crowded while the girls' room stayed eerily quiet. Was it normal? Having Coco included in our gang was therefore as natural as the law of supply and demand. What other choices did we have—hitting on a female teacher?

When it came to our turn, Coco had already been through two of our senior classes. Big Fly had nothing but disdain for her, and he called her a "loose woman." It was because of these words that Bulky Five wanted him dead. I also felt that it wasn't nice to call her that. To me, she was more like a mischievous big sister who was at once proud and gentle. The term "loose woman" was a bit outdated, not to mention the fact that Big Fly had never dated her.

Her coral bracelet was red in color. For untrained eyes, it might be mistaken for bloodstains from wrist slashing. She didn't always wear it: the bracelet would only appear on days when she was in a good mood. In summer when she was wearing short-sleeved dresses, the bracelet would look especially eye-catching, driving girls mad. In non-summer times, when she was wearing clothes with long sleeves, the on-again, off-again appearance of the bracelet could get men crazy, too. Once when we were hanging out, I wanted to feel the bracelet, and she got very angry and was about to strike me when Bulky Five jumped in, clutched my neck and warned, "Just remember, never lay a finger on Coco's bracelet."

Hell, he even used the expression "lay a finger on."

Coco said, "Come over, Bulky Five, I will let you feel it."

With sarcasm, Big Fly asked, "Feel where?"

Bulky Five again got into a fight with Big Fly. I have to confess, although Bulky Five was a foul-mouthed bastard and a bozo, his feeling for Coco was real and she was his goddess. Big Fly later commented, what goddamned goddess—at most she was a goddess of masturbation. Big Fly would surely die at the hands of Bulky Five if the latter overheard him.

I still remember clearly the fight between the Light Industry Vocational School and our class, a fight caused by two of their students making a pass at Coco. In order to save her and to let her know that she was now regarded as our girl, we all came out against the two unlucky devils. But before we even went into action, Bulky Five had picked up a brick and smashed the face of one of them and had the other one kneeling down before Coco and apologizing like a European gentleman. Coco was terrified and kept saying that we were courting bigger disaster. And sure enough, the next day more than a hundred of them rushed to our school and hit whomever they could lay their hands on.

Bulky Five was included in the unlucky group: he not only sustained visible wounds on his face, but also received administrative punishment from our school. He then made known his intention of gathering two hundred people to raze the Light Industry Vocation School to the ground. By then, Coco was ready to cut her ties to him once and for all.

"What kind of person is he anyway? A mental case?" Coco asked.

"He is just like that; he has a hormone disorder and can't control himself," Quiff explained. "He thinks of himself as a hero."

"But he would get me into big trouble," Coco protested. "He said that for me he was ready to die from a massive loss of blood!"

Quiff never believed in any of this nonsense. He said, "Gee, I have only seen women die from a massive loss of blood."

Coco left. We all sided with her and felt that Bulky Five went too far this time, except Big Fly, who reasoned, "Bulky Five may be a real bozo, but he did get beaten up because of Coco. Without us coming out to defend her, Coco would have been groped in public, and now she called Bulky Five a mental case. I think this woman is the one with mental problems. I am deeply disappointed in her."

Bulky Five failed to get the two hundred people he wanted.

In fact, in his rage he could be as crazy as two hundred people put together, so why didn't he go to the Vocational School alone, challenge them all and then die of massive hemorrhage? That way he would be remembered forever by Coco for his heroic act, and live in Coco's heart as a seventeen-year-old forever, or he could turn into a bead of her coral bracelet and stay bloody red forever.

Even in those violent and unlucky days, there were moments of calm and quiet, as well. For several months, there were neither thugs nor girls around. To kill time, we had no choice but to play mahjong. While playing mah-jongg, our talks would invariably turn to girls, such as Noisy, Icy and Broody. But we never talked about Coco, lest Bulky Five get too excited.

Big Fly's home was usually the place we played mahjong, but Bulky Five invited us over one time. Actually, he was not a good mahjong player, and not much a video game player, either. Simply put, he was not made to play games of any kind, except his life. In order not to hurt his feeling, we accepted his invitation.

At his home we met his father, a metalworker with impressive biceps and a head that looked like a kitchen chopper, hence we gave him the nickname "Chopper Head" in private. As a gracious host, he not only let us play mahjong, but also treated us each to a Red Pagoda Mountain cigarette. He didn't know the game either, but he was satisfied with being an observer and pleased to have a son who was apparently popular among friends. But when he later found out that we were playing with real money, he got angry and admonished us, "Young people should stay away from gambling!"

"Young people should stay away from a lot of things, smoking for instance," I said.

Chopper Head's response was: "Well, you will learn smoking sooner or later, but you should never gamble. Even after you get married, your women will not agree to let you gamble."

So we said to him, "Uncle, we will not play with real money then, just play for the fun of it, OK?"

"You should learn to be good kids," Chopper Head said.

"Yes, sir. Yes, sir."

When Bulky Five was out to buy beer, we chatted with Chopper Head about morality problems of juveniles as we continued to play. We weren't sure about his stand on the matter. He encouraged us to smoke, but also regarded fighting as rogue behavior. Besides, he also declared that if Bulky Five was ever involved in criminal behaviors he would have no compunction in beating his only son to death. It seemed that the more we talked, the more confused we became. We later concluded that Bulky Five inherited his neurotic behavior from his father.

Our topic then turned to the knife scar on Bulky Five's hand. We meant to praise his bravery, but also to remind Chopper Head that his son was not exactly one of those so-called "nice kids." To our surprise, Chopper Head listened and roared with laughter.

"I was the one who did that to him!"

"What?" We all raised our voices in shock.

Chopper Head explained, "He played hooky one day in junior high and I cut his hand with the chopper. That's how it happened."

Quiff shook his head, "A father who could cut the hand of his own son is something unheard of."

"I was really mad at him. Junior high students are not supposed to skip classes, am I right? He had good grades in elementary school, and I was hoping that he could go to college one day. Skipping classes landed him in the Chemical Engineering Technical School, instead, and one day he will become a metalworker like me."

Big Fly said, "What's the point of mentioning the grade school days now? I was one of the class leaders back in those days. All of us will become metalworkers one day."

Bulky Five showed up with a case of beer at this juncture and heard his father's complaint. He put the beer down and stared at Chopper Head across the mahjong table, but the latter didn't seem to have noticed his reaction. I said, "So your hand was actually scarred by your father. You can lie to us, but how could you lie to Coco, the woman you most admire?" Foreseeing trouble ahead, Big Fly stood up and stepped aside. Seeing the look on Bulky Five's face, I also beat my retreat in a hurry as Bulky Five pounced at Chopper Head and swore at him more than two hundred times across the mahjong table. Outraged, Chopper Head threw a chair at Bulky Five's head. Mahjong tiles flew everywhere like fireworks, and we tried to calm them down in turns, until they fought their way to the balcony. Obviously, Bulky Five had grown up and could now match his father in physical strength. We became mere spectators.

When Bulky Five finally wrestled Chopper Head to the ground, Quiff remarked, "I have never seen a son so brazenly thrashing his own father."

Bad news travels fast, and within a day, everybody knew that the scar on Bulky Five's hand was the work of his father. Coco sat on the wooden horse at the children's amusement park, eating an ice cream, and laughed her head off. Coco said, "Boys of your age so love to brag."

When Bulky Five showed up in school with his satchel, others looked at him askance or greeted him with scorn. He kept his mouth shut. He didn't want to fight anyone this time, nor could he find someone who was willing to fight him. Feeling the scar on the back of his hand, he sat by the window and muttered, "I will let you know whom you are dealing with."

Coco continued her good laugh, until she fell from the wooden horse.

Two months later, four bimbos showed up at our school door; they were also eating ice creams. They were of different heights and weights, good-looking ones mixed with ugly ones. It was her bad luck that Coco, on her way to school, was wearing her coral bracelet. In a narrow lane about fifty meters from the school, she came face to face with these four bimbos. They grabbed her and asked, "Are you Coco?"

"No, I am not," Coco answered.

"Bullshit! You have the red coral bracelet on and you are not Coco?" They each slapped her on the face, slipped the bracelet off her wrist and triumphantly walked away.

By the time we saw Coco, she was crying so hard she was almost out of breath. Like a kindergarten girl, she was shivering in a crouched position, her hands and shoulders convulsing violently with every word she uttered.

"They robbed me of my bracelet!"

Quiff said, "That's what they were after, your bracelet."

Coco said, "I recognized one of them—she is Sima Ling from the Textile Vocational School!"

That name, the most terrifying name in 1991, stunned us all into total silence. Her father was sentenced to death, her brother had spent times at reeducation camps, and she also had the support of an army of hooligans whose fighting power was rumored to exceed that of the Navy SEALs Special Operations Forces. With the help of only two female students, she could raze our school in no time, because the most ferocious brother of our school happened to be a loyal fan of Sima Ling. We helped Coco to her feet, and after much comforting, she finally stopped crying, but she then made an excessive demand.

"Help me get my bracelet back."

We looked at each other in despair. Big Fly said, "If it is in the possession of another girl, I can get it back for you. If it is with Sima Ling ..."

Quiff said it outright, "I don't have the courage."

"Neither do I," I said.

Fancy Pants proposed, "Let's enlist the help of the police."

Coco responded, "You are really a useless bunch. If only Bulky Five were here."

Bulky Five was not around. It was the time when Chopper

Head got hit by a loose object flying out of a moving elevator car at his factory and became a spatula head. He suffered from hydrocephalus and was on his deathbed. Bulky Five was at his bedside every day.

Back in 1991 there was a strange rule: no matter what happened, so long as it was not a serious crime like rape, murder or fire, you don't bother the police. Involving the police would mean that you were ready to quit your no-gooder's life and become a tame college-track kid. Plus, which police station was going to send its men out for a coral bracelet? Unless, of course, your father happened to be the station chief. We huddled around Coco and had a long discussion. She finally lost her patience and scolded every one of us bitterly, saying that she would seek the help of her male classmates. We readily agreed; after all, they were a year older and more powerful. As to whether they had the guts to skin Sima Ling, we were not that optimistic.

To look for a bracelet, Quiff and I went to a souvenir market with a huge selection of coral trinkets. White corals were everywhere, including coral mountains or coral pen holders, but there were no red corals, nor were there bracelets. According to the shop owner, red corals were rare, probably from Hong Kong or Taiwan; even if they were around, they would be priced beyond our reach. On reflection, we decided he might have been right. If it were something readily available, why would the big shot Sima Ling bother to steal it from Coco?

Despondent, Quiff and I walked back. I felt that we truly cared about Coco. Although we were unable to get her bracelet back, we were willing to buy one for her, and that was a show of sincerity on our part. We stopped at the Textile Vocational School on the way, and saw Sima Ling sitting by herself on the edge of the platform on the campus grounds. Her hair blowing in the wind, she looked calm and elegant, not at all like the female terror she was. The red coral bracelet on her wrist seemed so eye-catching, so dazzling. If we rushed over and hit her with a brick, we would be able to get back the bracelet and win Coco over, but we couldn't. Sima Ling was also beautiful, same as Coco, and we were not supposed to strike a beautiful girl.

Bulky Five reappeared, wearing a black armband. Chopper Head had passed away.

"Don't let yourself overtaken by grief," we advised him.

Bulky Five said, "From now on, no one is going to hold me back anymore." He then learned about what happened to Coco, and said, "Just let this whole thing cool down a bit."

To show our understanding, we replied, "You are right, stay out of it. Your father just died."

I couldn't discern any grief on his part. He came and went as he always did, with a sullen face, to show how cool he was. Fancy Pants theorized that Bulky Five's silence proved that he was in grief. But Big Fly pointed out that Bulky Five had been kept to himself ever since that time we played mahjong.

Coco came to look for Bulky Five, and denounced every one of us in front of him: Big Fly is useless, Quiff is useless, Fancy Pants is useless, Lu Xiaolu is useless. We all looked shamefaced. Bulky Five broke into a smile, a very sinister smile, and said, "I got it." He then left.

Coco said, "Bulky Five is useless too."

It turned out that the bracelet incident was not over. Coco's birthday was coming, and she had long planned to have a birthday party when she would make her appearance in her most beautiful clothes that matched her bracelet. She got an impressive-looking boy of her class nicknamed Tiger, one of her admirers, to go to the Textile Vocational School alone as her negotiator. Tiger relayed Coco's offer: she was willing to buy back the bracelet with one hundred yuan and give Sima Ling a pearl necklace, to boot. Sima Ling responded by giving Tiger a good kick, then she patted Tiger's stubbly young face and said, "Come and be my movie companion tomorrow." That was how damn Tiger switched sides and became one of them.

A week passed, and when Coco's miserable birthday party

finally took place at a small dance hall, many people chose to stay away. It was a rundown place. The strobe light no longer turned in circles and the karaoke songs were all dated. Coco had asked every one of us to bring three bottles of beer, believing that at least twenty of our classmates would show up, but only Quiff and I made it. While we were drinking the beers we bought ourselves and Coco's face was turning green, Bulky Five came in.

He took the red coral bracelet from his trouser pocket and said to Coco, "I have wrestled it back for you." This was how he did it. He slipped into the Textile Vocational School in the afternoon and locked his eyes on Sima Ling; he then crouched in a corner and waited for her to be alone. As evening approached, she was alone, as we saw her last, when she came out on the school grounds for some fresh air. Bulky Five walked over, and totally unmoved by the serene-looking beauty, he grabbed her by the neck and removed the red coral bracelet from her wrist. Sima Ling struggled a little; Bulky Five clenched her hair and dragged her to the ground. He then sped away with all his might, climbed over the fence and ran directly to the dance hall, not even daring to retrieve his bicycle.

Our eyes were all on the bracelet and we were waiting for Coco to take it back and give Bulky Five a huge reward, maybe a kiss. But Coco was far smarter than we thought. She said, "This is it, you are a dead man now." At this moment, seven or eight men suddenly burst in from the front and back doors of the dance hall, grabbed Bulky Five, knocked him down, beat him up and pinned him face down on the table, right atop Coco's birthday cake. One of them took out a spring knife and stuck it right into his left buttock as if he were about to slice a cake.

All I remembered that day was Bulky Five's scream and Coco's squeal. As those blurry-faced guys left the scene, Bulky Five was still on top of the birthday cake, Coco had not stopped her wailing, "Bulky Five, you ruined my birthday party!"

No one knew the whereabouts of the red coral bracelet; neither

Coco nor Sima Ling had it. It disappeared in the brawl. Maybe some bastards swiped it, but this was no longer important.

In those days we talked about all kinds of knife wounds. I knew of instances of people's bellies being knifed through—that was vicious. But mostly the stories were softer and lighthearted, such as an unlucky guy who got knifed in the buttocks in a fight. You know that those who wield knives usually are not willing to become murderers of petty nobodies, not when a stab in the rear would do. Of course, sometimes even that could become a life-threatening wound, say, if the knife poked the femoral artery. That's bad luck; after all, the knife-wielders were ruffians, not surgeons.

Bulky Five didn't die. He was rushed to the No. 2 Peoples' Hospital with the knife sticking out of his rear. The doctor asked us what happened, we gave him the story that he sat on the knife by mistake. The doctor said, "Bah! Don't you think I know that he was stabbed?" After the surgery, Bulky Five insisted that the doctor return the spring knife to him and it stayed in his satchel ever after.

Bulky Five of the Tech School class of '89 thus became known as the most brilliant, ominous star and the messenger of death, who actually had two scary-looking knife scars on his body. The one inflicted by his father was on his hand, and the location of the other scar was more private, and not appropriate for public display. At certain moments, such as when the name Coco was mentioned in our conversation, his face would still betray a strange emotion, a mixture of pride and melancholy, followed by his staring at the scar on his raised hand. Big Fly would remind him time and again: please, the scar caused by Coco is on your behind.

One day, Tiger also came to chat with us. He half-jokingly said, "Bulky Five, Coco is so afraid of you now. Because you were too ferocious, you even dared to attack Sima Ling. If you continue to be ferocious, Coco will be in trouble."

With his eyes fixed on Tiger, Bulky Five said, "You tell me, who among us is really the useless one."

Annoyed, Tiger said, "OK, I am useless, we are all useless, and you are the only exception. Are you satisfied? But, please, don't make any more trouble for Coco. The red coral bracelet is now gone, and Coco has no intention of getting stabbed one day because of it."

Even Sima Ling sent in two hundred yuan through an intermediary to cover part of the medical expenses. Ever since she learned that she was dealing with a reckless one, she also worried that she might be knifed on her behind one day when she happened to be all by herself. She was a woman, after all. Bulky Five accepted the money and said in a low voice, "I would never use a knife against a woman."

Big Fly said, "Come on, it was you who held her by her hair. You thought you were the knight in shining armor. Sima Ling is much more mature than Coco, also more beautiful."

Bulky Five said, "I only care for Coco, and it was she who asked me to get her bracelet back."

Big Fly remarked calmly, "She wanted you to get her bracelet back, but she didn't want to be burned by the fire. Maybe you should have killed Sima Ling on the campus ground and then return the bracelet to Coco. For that you would receive the death penalty and she would be cleared of any connections to the crime, would you do that?"

We were loitering around all day and doing nothing. The days when we chased around the young girl Coco were gone forever, since she soon joined a saccharine plant as an apprentice. Later we came to know many girls, including the street girl Noisy and the Textile Vocational School girl Broody, and they filled the place left by the cold-hearted Coco. Bulky Five would join us from time to time, but he wasn't popular among the girls. He used to be a blustering and hot-blooded guy, but after the stabbing incident he turned quiet and kept to himself. No one actually liked him. Once when talking about scars, Broody said, "You are all useless. None of you have ever been stabbed." Big Fly then related the story of Bulky Five. Broody said, "To have a scar buried on the buttocks is truly a damn nuisance—the wife will be the only one he can show it off to."

The story is about to come to an end, but not quite. That fall, our Coco returned to the Chemical Engineering Technical School after five months of apprenticeship. Her belly was showing—she was pregnant, and it didn't seem that she intended to have an abortion, so the school had her dismissed. With the letter of dismissal in hand, she walked past us, beaming in bliss. We called out and asked, "Hey, Coco, who is the father of your child?" She just smiled and kept walking.

A chemistry teacher cried out after Coco, "Bitch!" She didn't turn her head at that remark, either, and kept walking. I saw Bulky Five softly sigh without uttering a word. The chemistry teacher was stabbed by a masked man in an alley the night after. He was knifed at the buttocks, and no one knew who did it.

The First Generation ID Card

More than twenty years ago, we were all playing video games on the so-called "street machine." The biggest game room in town was called Blue State, where in addition to video games, you could also lease game cards used on Nintendo game machines. Around this time, the first generation ID cards had just been issued, and the owner of Blue State decided to allow leasing of the game cards with no money down, just the ID cards of the players. He probably believed that an ID card was a very important item one cannot do without. That was what we believed, as well, though it was a belief apparently not everyone shared.

To be more specific, there were people who used their IDs to lease game cards and then never returned. Even if they returned, it would be almost impossible for the owner to match their faces with the piles of cards left behind. With time, Blue State's front counter was covered all over with ID cards of the garbage kids who had nothing but time to kill. The owner finally realized that asking for deposits was the way to go; ID cards were worth nothing, since you could always claim you lost yours and ask for a replacement. In those days, game cards were valued at about a hundred yuan, but I can't recall the deposit Blue State charged.

One day, the owner of Blue State asked Yang Chi and me over. We had been playing the Contra game on the Nintendo machine there, at two yuan an hour and ten yuan all night, and had probably played about five hundred hours altogether. That was where we spent most of our summer holiday. Even after we went back home, the images of the game still floated and lingered in our brains. The owner asked if we would be willing to use the ID cards to get the game cards back, and with every returned game card we would be given three nights of Nintendo playing for free. That seemed to be a win-win deal, since the store needed more all-night gamers and we had spent all our pocket money for the summer. The owner added that he should have asked for the money they owed, as these bastards all owed at least a hundred yuan to the store, but after consideration he had decided to give them a break. I thought it was a good idea, since asking for the game cards back was not as dangerous as asking for the money back.

Yang Chi and I were both seventeen at the time. As a technical school student who had a bunch of friends ready to fight on my behalf, I was not someone to be trifled with. Of course, their help came at a heavy price—I had to help them out when they were in need. As for Yang Chi, he was an A student at a "key school," and ranked top three in science. He was averse to fights and was addicted to detective stories. Incidentally, his uncle worked at the prosecutor's office.

As we left with a handful of IDs and the receipts with their signatures, we cursed the damn fatso owner of Blue State, a dwarfish but shrewd fellow, for using us to his own advantage. We got on our bikes and headed toward the West Ring Village, where five of the ID card owners resided.

We encountered problems almost from the very beginning. A big and husky boy named Wang Yong punched me right in front of his home and also managed to wrestle his ID back; another boy named Guo Jianguo was playing games at home with three other boys, and Yang Chi and I immediately made our escape downstairs before he even made his move against us. We ended up drinking cola in front of the village general store. While I felt the part of my face that was hurting, Yang Chi was flipping through the IDs in his hands out of boredom. He cried out all of a sudden, "Hey, there is a girl."

According to the information shown on the ID, she was born on Jan. 31, 1972, so she was a year older than us. Usually the big-headed ID photos were most unflattering, making normal human beings look more like ghosts, but she seemed innocent and pure, with shoulder-length hair, bright eyes and a cute-looking, slightly upturned nose. We studied this picture closely under the scorching sun and finally decided to visit her next. Her name was Liu Qinghua.

It was the last row of the village buildings to the south of the river. Camphor trees, the most common sight in our city, were planted everywhere in the village. But what stood guard behind the last row of buildings were five willow trees next to the river. I don't care about willow trees, because they carry slug caterpillars in summer and look horrifying in winter. We walked into the completely dark stairway cramped with household stuff and went straight up to the fifth floor.

"I like the name Liu Qinghua," Yang Chi remarked. "I will succeed in the entrance exam and get into Qinghua (also known as Tsinghua University) next summer."

"Too bad your name is Yang Chi," I said.

We found Liu Qinghua's apartment number and knocked on the door. A middle-aged man answered the door. He looked odd with the clothes he had on, only a jacket covering his bare chest. In those days people often used the factory-issued uniform as a jacket and wore it everywhere. But it was summer, the hottest season of the year, and only an idiot would wear that to relax at home.

We explained that we were there for Liu Qinghua, whose ID card was used as a deposit for a box of twenty game cards two months ago.

The man said, "Liu Qinghua went out at noon. She doesn't play video games. Two months ago she was preparing for the college entrance examination—how could she find time to play games? I only knew that she lost her ID earlier this year, so someone else must have used it instead."

Yang Chi explained, "But at Blue State the one who leases the game card has to be the person shown on the ID."

The man replied, "I have no idea anyway, let me ask Liu Qinghua when she comes back."

Yang Chi asked, "And what is your relationship to her?"

The man answered, "I am her father."

He closed the door. The man sounded tough, and might be a difficult one to deal with. To tangle with adults on their turf would get us into unnecessary trouble. So we had no choice but to leave. As we reached the third floor, Yang Chi stopped and said, "This old bastard had not been forthcoming with us. Did you notice his lower body? It was popped up."

I confessed, "No, I didn't."

Yang Chi said, "It was popped up, even under cover of his long pants. You just didn't look down."

I said, "Haven't you ever heard the idiom 'to indulge oneself sexually in broad daylight'?"

Yang Chi replied, "Never learned it."

"Don't worry, it will never show up on the entrance exam," I said.

As we lingered, we heard footsteps coming down, and it was Liu Qinghua's father trying to catch up with us. I took a look at his lower body; it was no longer popped up. He stopped in front of Yang Chi and said, "Give me her ID."

"You return the game cards and I will give you the ID," Yang Chi responded.

That sent him into a rage, and he grabbed Yang Chi by the collar and asked, "You two no-gooders, what were you trying to do with my daughter's ID?" He slapped Yang Chi in the face and with that Yang's glasses flew out of the stairway window. This old bastard really needed a sound beating. A brawl ensued. The stairway was hot and the afternoon was quiet, as people had all gone back to work. After a while we realized that all our blows on our opponent were more like massages for him, but his initial slap was whipped with real force. Finally, he clutched Yang Chi's neck with his two fingers and, while my feeble fists never stopped punching him, reached for the ID cards in Yang Chi's pocket. Jumping at the opportunity, Yang Chi quickly landed his fist on his eyes. Like playing cards, all the ID cards went flying.

We had to pick them all up, because every one of them had a box of game cards behind it. When I stooped to do that, this nearly deranged man gave me an unexpected kick to the head. I lost balance and fell from the stairs. He then used a hook to throw Yang Chi down as well.

"I am a metalworker," the man covered his eyes and said arrogantly, "you little tramps are no match for me. I would have no problem with five more of you. Just get out of my sight."

Yang Chi and I fled from the building. We had now lost all the ID cards, or to put it another way, all the game cards. We sat down under the willow tree. I took off my undershirt and pressed it against my bleeding head wound. Yang Chi stooped by the river to wash away the blood around his mouth. We looked utterly defeated.

"What do we say when we return to Blue State?"

"What do we say?" Yang Chi answered, "We ask the boss to pay for our medical costs."

"Damn it, I still have to get the ID cards back."

When we returned to the building, the man was gone. A girl was holding a stack of ID cards in her hand and was about to come downstairs. She stopped when she saw me and said, "All the IDs are here, except mine. I am Liu Qinghua."

She was pretty, really, even prettier than her ID photo. Her skin was white as snow and her hair shiny black. But she was not the pure and innocent type I liked. Her eyes were tinged heavily with blood.

"The one who attacked us, is he your father?"

"Yes," she said slowly, as if she was held back or got confused in reflection, or her memory had completely failed her. "He attacked you."

I opened my palm and raised my hand as if I was making a pledge, so that she could see it from the landing. I was holding an ID card, the one I picked up before I was kicked on the head. It was hers. The one I picked up at random turned out to be her ID. I was bare-chested, my other hand still clutching the undershirt against my head, and it seemed that blood was still gushing from the wound.

She said, "Give it back to me!" She raised her head toward the stairway and called out, "Daddy!"

Yang Chi walked over, took the blood-smeared ID from my hand and waved it at her. "You and your father are having an incestuous relationship," he said.

She cried out, "Daddy!"

Yang Chi and I stepped back, but before leaving I said to her, "You can have all those IDs, but we will have yours. I will look at it often, Liu Qinghua. Go ask your father to fight me then."

No One Was Innocent

It was a short stint of internship in June. We worked at an institute specializing in metal processing, including the slicing, chopping and pressing of all kinds of metals. The institute was far from town, and the rest of my classmates were all assigned to the much more interesting chemical engineering plant; Big Fly and I were the only ones assigned here. At first we were envious of others, but we later became the objects of their envy, as the institute might be boring, but it was clean and neat; plus, no one in particular was specifically in charge of us. Big Fly and I would report to duty every day to the section chief named Liao, use the bench vice in the workshop to work unhurriedly on some metal pieces in the morning and then have the whole afternoon to ourselves. Conversely, those classmates assigned to work in the chemical engineering plant would all be dog-tired by the end of the day.

At the time, we were students of "maintenance" in the Chemical Engineering Technical School class of '89, but we had no idea how to repair things, and we were not taught how to do it, either. We were tasked with studying mostly fine arts subjects, including Chinese, math, politics and mechanical drawing. After a while, even I felt the need to know what kind of tool a "file" was.

Big Fly and I often slipped out. There wasn't that much to see in the neighborhood. Weeds seemed to be particularly invasive, like noise, in June. With the sun burning above and the earth baked dry, dust was everywhere. But you knew that the worst was yet to come; this was only the beginning, and things would get really crazy in August.

Chen Guozhen came to see how we were doing. Chen Guozhen was our class supervisor, a man in his thirties but still unmarried, hence a bit depressed. The black wool coat he had on in winter made him looked super cool, to the point that the thought of knocking him down in the alley and wearing that coat to see Dandan, the girl I liked, had even crossed my mind several times. But this happened to be summertime, and Chen Guozhen looked downright unimpressive in summer. He didn't seem to have many shirt choices, and was wearing a police-style shirt readily available from street vendors. Back in the 1990s, these police shirt lookalikes sold by street vendors were very popular, and you would sometimes see a bunch of people wearing police shirts arresting another bunch of people wearing the same shirts. I never wore them; they had this screwed-up look that would reduce my mum to tears.

Chen Guozhen said to Big Fly and me, "F--k you, how did you manage to get apprenticeship at such a nice place? I will arrange to have you two work at a sulphur plant next month."

"Teacher Chen, the sulphur plant is so far away," I said.

"This place is also far away from town, f--k you," Chen Guozhen said.

This place was not that far away for Big Fly though, since he lived in a village just outside the railway bridge. It was considered a high-crime area. Desperate out-of-towners along the main road stopped at nothing for a living: they stole bicycles, manhole covers, communication cables and whatever else they could lay their hands on. This occurred so often that even local big shots like Big Fly found it a bit out of control.

Chen Guozhen also asked Section Chief Liao for more information. Chief Liao knew us quite well by now, and his wife used to be the section head of the workshop my father was in, so he put in some nice words for me. For instance, I was eager to help others and also very polite. Chen Guozhen was staring at me as if he was looking at an alien. But Chief Liao soon made a slip, "Lu Xiaolu also treated me to cigarettes from time to time." Chen Guozhen said, "F--k you, as a Tech School student, you will be punished for smoking, and you even dared to treat others to cigarettes?"

I said, "I am merely doing what the local custom dictates, Teacher Chen."

Chen Guozhen said, "You are such damn good material for a worker, f--k you."

And then, Chief Liao and Chen Guozhen started chatting. They talked about the worsening security situation: thievery was so rampant, even the institute was not spared. People would scale the fence and steal metal blocks, bars and plates. If this should continue, Big Fly and I would soon have no metal to work on at all. The institute had only limited number of personnel; even Chief Liao himself was in the rotation for night duty. He was hoping that Big Fly and I would also join in the rotation, since we seemed tough, good at fighting and fearless. Chen Guozhen said, "F--k you, where are the police when you need them? If the police were doing their job as they should, more than half of my class would be arrested. It would be nice if they would arrest them all." Chen Guozhen added later, "You need to keep an eye on these two students. They may not have stolen metal blocks, but if my memory serves me, they have stolen oranges and broken the ribs of the store owner."

Big Fly, who had kept quiet all the while finally murmured "f--k you" in a low voice.

Chen Guozhen then left with Chief Liao for a few drinks. At noon, Big Fly and I flipped over the wall for some fresh air. We both agreed that failure to have barbed wire on top of the low wall was causing the theft. But this was not of our concern; it would be better if all the metal blocks were stolen. I found the noise of metal cutting extremely unpleasant, probably the most terrible sound in the world.

We walked on the narrow cement pavement surrounded by weeds and trees. The pavement was next to the wall at the beginning, but they gradually parted ways, with the pavement extending farther into the weed-covered ground. Big Fly said that going in the opposite direction would lead us to places with more human activity, places we passed every day on our way to the institute. But what was there to explore in familiar grounds? Nothing. We preferred to explore unfamiliar grounds, instead. After quite a long walk, the road became unpaved dirt road, you could hear the train passing and the railway was in sight ahead of us, partly hidden by the redwood trees. Whenever a train passed, the trees would quaver in rhythm. We finally reached the railroad bridge; underneath the bridge was total darkness. What lay beyond the darkness?

"There is nothing beyond that," Big Fly answered.

This is ridiculous, how could there be nothing ahead of us? There must be something. We couldn't possibly reach the end of the world in such a short time.

Big Fly said, "You would enter the area of shantytown, where all kinds of strange out-of-towners reside."

"The out-of-towners are terrible people," I said. "They would steal anything."

We squatted under the railway bridge for a smoke, staring at the underpass as if a bunch of out-of-towners might pop up at any time. I found the thought amusing, since once in a while Big Fly and I made off with a few things as well, such as fruits and cigarettes; the biggest theft we had committed was a bicycle. But now we were considered ourselves upright citizens, and the out-of-towners on the other side of the underpass bona fide thieves.

Lost in thought, Big Fly stretched out his arm and plucked a flower from a roadside fence.

"You are not allowed to pluck my flowers."

We turned and looked at this young man in a wheelchair, eyes full of hatred. In town this expression could cost him his life, but the other side of the railroad bridge was way too bleak and wild, and also he was in a wheelchair.

Big Fly arrogantly made a half turn and with his ear facing the young man he asked, "What did you just say?"

"You are not allowed to touch my pumpkin flowers," he said.

Big Fly looked at the yellow flower in his hand. "Ah, this

is a pumpkin flower. Plucking a pumpkin flower is the same as plucking a pumpkin, is it what you were saying?"

"Exactly," he said. He had an accent that marked him as a non-local.

I sized up the living quarters behind him. It was a lean-to built against the railroad bridge, propped up by bamboo sticks and covered by a sheet of black tarp. The inside of the shed was obscured by darkness. Only out-of-towners would reside in such bamboo sheds. The pumpkin was grown on a makeshift fence.

I then looked at his wheelchair, which had been created by adding two wheels to a chair; it was a shoddy piece of work, but served its purpose. Both of his legs were in casts.

"Did you break your legs?" I asked.

"It's none of your business," he said. "Just get out of my sight, this is my home."

"If I ate one of your pumpkin seeds, would you think that I have consumed twenty of your pumpkins?" With a smile, Big Fly was still trying to taunt him with words.

"By fall, it will become a pumpkin," the young man insisted, pointing at the flower.

"By winter, it will become a f--king nothing," Big Fly retorted in a shout.

I told Big Fly to let it go, that a shouting match was not going to accomplish anything. "Do you really want to fight with a 14- or 15-year-old boy with two broken legs and a foreign accent by the railroad bridge underpass? You were once at his age, you know very well that boys at that age are all stubborn, stupid and believe that they own the whole world." I was more than familiar with those eyes of hatred; it was at once an expression of his true emotion and a show. All the punks were very good at wearing that expression, which was actually worth nothing.

At this juncture, a train happened to roar past the bridge over our head. During its passage, no words were exchanged between us. Then Big Fly walked toward him and kicked a few times at his wheels, and the young man with the broken legs retreated.

"Don't you touch me!" he screamed.

Big Fly continued his kicks against his wheels, "I will touch you, touch you, touch you."

Obviously, he got on Big Fly's nerves. Big Fly always regarded himself as a cool guy, and he rarely lost his temper. With my back to the fence, I lit a cigarette and watched Big Fly fly into a rage and wrestle the broken-legged boy to the ground and tap his toe against the boy's head. The boy screamed and crawled along the ground, and then he flipped over and tried to bite Big Fly. Big Fly darted away, but continued his taunting.

"That's enough, Big Fly, let's go," I said.

"Come and give me a hand."

"You are fighting someone with two broken legs, and you need my help?"

"Help me to throw his wheelchair into the river."

"You might as well break his leg again."

Immediately I heard the anguished shriek of the young man. By this time, he had crawled to the entrance of the bamboo shed. With a dismissive smile, Big Fly eased his way in, too. I then heard a cry of surprise from him in the dark, "Damn it, metal blocks of the institute are everywhere." I followed him in. After a temporary blindness and a brief period of adjustment, piles of metal blocks, bars and plates from the institute, with red painted numbers intact, emerged right in front my eyes. Besides the loot I also saw two beds; no, strictly speaking, they were not beds, but places you could lie down. The last time the bed sheets were washed was probably a hundred years ago. Many flying insects flitted around in the rays coming through the chinks in the wall. I don't know who could have slept here or how could anyone even lie down here.

"You had the nerve to complain that I plucked your pumpkin flower." Big Fly walked over to grab the young man. "You are a thief. I will report you to the police."

After looking at Big Fly for quite some time, the young man lying on the ground realized that it was time for him to ask for mercy.

"Please let me off this time," he said.

Big Fly couldn't hear him, and once again turned his ear toward him and even stretched out his hand to pat on the boy's face a few times. This time, the boy no longer dared to bite him in response.

"Uncle, I am calling you uncles, please let me off."

Big Fly raised his neck a few times in my direction. Yes, my judgment of character turned out to be wrong; the boy was not stubborn, or stupid, nor did he believe that he owned the whole world; the boy actually was quite damn sophisticated. Out of frustration I walked over and also gave him a kick.

Big Fly pulled me back. As I raised my head I saw a group of men with iron bars approaching, spaced out like flying geese, from the other side of the fence. I counted, and there were six of them. The boy immediately howled.

It is better for me to spare you the details of what happened next. What came to my mind later were all bloodstained scenes. They had Big Fly kneeling on the ground, totally under their control. The young man from his sitting position slapped him dozens of times, then he told the others that their thievery was now exposed. One of the men who dragged Big Fly into the shed was heard in a loud discussion with others in the back if we two should be bludgeoned to death and the shed set on fire. The others sounded hesitant. Big Fly was heard crying out loud, "Uncle, just let me off please." At the time I was being trampled underfoot, half of my face buried in the ground, and I was unable to speak.

I admit this was the most perilous situation I ever encountered at age seventeen, but this was nothing; later in my life I have faced similar situations. Once someone pointed a knife next to my waist area, another time a firearm was pointed at my head. Such instances were few in number, but were enough for bragging purposes to my friends. I only learned later that bludgeoned to death was a terrible way to die. It's a painful process to go through, since the ones who do the bludgeoning might not crack your cranium on the first hit, but might choose to go slowly and crack every bone in your body one at a time and turn you into a snake. If Big Fly and I didn't die of our wounds they would probably have us burned into ashes, like barbeque meat. Our bodies would be found burned black and curled. I wondered what those girls who knew us would say in their remembrance of us and whether pumpkins would grow on our graves.

That very day I heard a bicycle bell ringing and a voice shouting, "What are you doing!" The foot that held me to the ground suddenly was gone; I only managed to get back on my own feet after lying on the ground for a long while. Those men were no longer in sight, nor was the boy with two broken legs (Big Fly told me later that he escaped on someone's back along with the others). Chen Guozhen stood in front of us, and he was drunk, his police shirt unbuttoned at three places. Sitting on a bicycle with one foot on the ground, and with his fingers pointing at us, he asked, "F--k you, you two were involved in street fighting again, yes or no?"

"Teacher Chen," Big Fly said in sobs, "Teacher Chen, you looked so damn much like a policeman."

"F--k you," Chen Guozhen said.

When we returned to the institute in the afternoon, Big Fly and I were utterly exhausted, and his face was swollen out of shape. Chief Liao came over and checked on us, and he let us talk to the station police about what happened and the shed stuffed with stolen goods. Big Fly sounded miserable and his voice trembled. The police tried to allay his fear, "Rest assured, you will never run into these people again, unless you also get yourself in jail."

Chief Liao said, "I was on patrol duty last week when a boy tried to climb over and I poked him back to the other side of the wall with an iron bar, and I heard him lying there crying in pain. I figure he must be the one you met with the broken legs."

After thinking for a long while, my mind just drew a total blank. I said, "Right, it must be him, I am sure. He was a very dangerous, criminal."

Keep Running, Little Brother

My little brother, Wu Shuangfeng, was born in 1984. The day he was born, Dad was doing overtime at the factory. Nan and Granddad were at home playing mahjong. The baby had shown up on the ultrasound as a girl, so Dad's side of the family wasn't particularly bothered about the birth. They already had one girl, me, and having another would be a complete waste of our child quota; we wouldn't be able to try again even if we wanted to. But when the baby was born it turned out to be a boy, and what's more, he had pneumonia of newborn. When Grandpa, Mum's father, called up to tell Dad the news, he threw down his electrician's knife and rushed over to the hospital. He twisted his ankle jumping off the bus at Xujiahui, and by the time he arrived the baby was in intensive care and no one could see him.

So how did Shuangfeng become a boy? As a child it really puzzled me. I only really understood when I got to university. Ultrasound scans can be unreliable. The foetus sometimes keeps his little penis hidden, and so the doctor decides it's a girl. Nowadays it's against the law to do "non-medical checks" to determine the sex, but at some hospitals if you slip them a sweetener they'll scan you on the sly. Sometimes, if it shows up as a girl, the parents will decide to have an abortion, but then it turns out to have been a boy all along. This ambivalence around the birth would prove a sign that life for my brother wasn't going to be easy. You see, Granddad Wu had wanted to have my brother aborted and Dad refused to take sides, but my mother's side of the family was adamant we should keep the baby, which is the only reason he's here at all.

As a baby, Shuangfeng was always ill. It was as if his resistance had been all but used up by that bout of pneumonia. We had no idea exactly how many IV bags and how much antibiotics he had been given during his stay in intensive care. He had spent the first part of his life shielded from view behind a white curtain, but as he grew bigger we could see he had slanted eyes, a raised-up upper lip permanently parted from the lower one, a dark complexion, and six toes on his left foot. As children we would sit on the steps outside East China Normal University's staff dormitory and count our toes. I had ten but he had eleven, no matter how many times we counted. With his raised-up lip, he couldn't keep saliva from dribbling out all over them. He was four at the time, and naively thought that everyone was born with eleven toes. "No, Shuangfeng, ten toes, not eleven," I would tell him. He didn't believe me, but when we went hand-in-hand to ask Granny, she mournfully pronounced, "Most people have ten toes, Shuangfeng. You have a birth defect."

Grandpa was a professor at East China Normal University. He came up with my brother's name. In Grandpa's home village there was a river, the Twin Moon, and as I was born in February, the second month of the year, I was named "Twin Moon," or Shuangyue, after the river. As it happened, there was also a mountain near the village called the "Twin Peaks." Grandpa thought, as "Twin Moon" was such a good girl's name, why not call the boy "Twin Peaks," or Shuangfeng, after the mountain. This carefully thought out yet utterly careless idea completely destroyed my brother. "Twin Peaks"—you might as well call him two-humped Bactrian camel or make some boob jokes, and what with having a surname like Wu, a homophone for "nothing," the possibilities for nicknames were endless. The fact is, the whole time I was growing up, I never heard his friends call him by his real name.

The whole family doted on my brother. As the only third-generation son and heir it was only natural. We weren't badly off. Dad was promoted from electrician to workshop chief. Mum worked on a government job. We could afford whatever we wanted. Shuangfeng might have been the pet at home, but he was never taken out of the house. Mum and Dad always took me when their work units organized holiday tours, dressing it up as "Shuangfeng's too young," when in fact they thought he would be an embarrassment to them. When we looked back at our childhood, it turned out I'd been to most of China's famous sites, whereas Shuangfeng had always stayed home with Granny and Grandpa during numerous summer and winter holidays. "I don't want to talk about it," he would say later on. Even when Granny went out food shopping, if at all possible, she would take me rather than Shuangfeng.

You can't run very fast with an extra toe, so when Shuangfeng was five he had an operation to remove it. My parents thought maybe he'd be able to run better, but as it turned out, he had flat feet as well so it didn't make much difference. Growing up, I lost count of the times I saw other boys going after him. He would run for his life on those once eleven-toed and forever flat feet, tears and dribble flying. I'm five years older so I would charge over to stop them. Then one day, on my way home with some classmates, I saw a group of girls pushing him about. They were shrieking, pulling his hair, pinching his ears, and yanking at his school bag. Nine-year-old Shuangfeng sat on the ground in tears, trying to escape and screaming at them to stop. I took out my steel ruler and whacked the little demons over the head. They backed off. This time it was my turn to be teased.

"Wu Shuangyue, is that your brother Wu Shuangfeng?"

"Come here, Wu Shuangfeng, and let me have a look at you."

"Your little brother's really ugly."

"How could you let yourself be bullied by girls?" I asked him. "They ganged up on me," he said, wiping away tears. I sighed, said goodbye to my friends and took his hand in mine and went home. On the way home he suddenly looked at me. "Your friends know about me?" he asked. "Yes," I said. "And they know my name is Wu Shuangfeng?" My heart trembled. I had made jokes about Shuangfeng to a few close friends, it was true. Even though they'd never met him, he was well-known because of that stupid name.

Seeing that I wasn't going to answer, he didn't press further. Walking on he said suddenly, "I'll get my own back when I'm older." After a while, he added, "I'll get my revenge on those girls."

I looked at him, he was the same old slant-eyed, goofy-mouthed boy. He still had a tear in the corner of his eye. "I doubt you'll ever get a girl looking like that," I thought to myself, "let alone get your revenge."

My brother had a miserable childhood. Even in year five, he was still dribbling over his homework. The family was always scolding him, "Close your mouth, Shuangfeng!" Even the maid started doing it. I wouldn't stand for that, so I falsely accused her of stealing and got her dismissed. I wasn't surprised he got low marks at school; he had no confidence in himself. The few times he did well, the teacher assumed that he must have been cheating, and for that Mum and Dad gave him a thrashing. He cried his heart out, but nothing he said could persuade them otherwise, his explanation would be interpreted as additional lies on his part. He was thus known to be a low-achiever, a cheater and a liar. "I'm stuck whatever I do," he told me. He was only twelve at the time.

That wasn't the only traumatic experience of my brother's life: in year two he was forced to undergo a circumcision at school. Some doctors came into class and examined all the boys, but it was only Shuangfeng whose foreskin they decided was too long. They took him to the clinic and sliced it off there and then. Smearing on some antiseptic, they told him not to drink fluids or pee, and then sent him back to class. Able to bear it at first, it soon hurt so much he couldn't sit down. Then he got told off for crying. By the end he was clutching at his penis, and jumping up and down. At that point they called Mum to take him off their hands. Shuangfeng was still crying when we sat down for dinner. My dad got angry, the school had gone too far this time. Why wasn't the head of the family informed? I asked Granny what a foreskin was as I ate my dinner. "That's not the sort of thing a girl should ask," she mournfully replied. "Shuangyue, I think your brother has probably been gelded." I have to say, at this point, that Granny had let her imagination run away with her. Though I was once convinced there was something wrong with my brother's physiognomy, I learned at university that circumcision can be a good thing, but why be so brutal about it?

After finishing junior high, Shuangfeng wanted to go to culinary institute to become a chef. This wasn't good enough for a learned family like ours. Grandpa owned a huge collection of books, could recite classical poems and write Ou-style (after Ouyang Xiu, a famous scholar of the Song Dynasty) calligraphy, how could he possibly tolerate his only grandson working in a restaurant? He was so put out, he hardly ate for days. He scolded Dad at mealtimes, until he lost his appetite as well. Then Dad turned on Shuangfeng. The dinner table became a battlefield. In the end Granny said mournfully, "Shuangfeng, you can't close your mouth. What if you dribble all over the food?" "Granny, I don't dribble anymore," replied my brother, aggrieved, "haven't you even noticed?" It wasn't entirely Granny's fault. Shuangfeng still couldn't close his mouth properly, so whether he was at the age of fifteen, twenty or even after he was twenty-four, whenever he was caught lost in thought, the family would still remind him strictly, gently, or matter-of-factly to close his mouth.

Anyhow, he went on to senior high, where he focused all his energy on getting into university. A lot of people think the university entrance exam pass rate is high in Shanghai compared with other places. But from my experience I would say that it might be true since two thirds of junior high graduates who have already been channeled into vocational or technical schools were excluded from that statistics. Culinary institute would have been a good option considering his lousy marks, but pushed into following the college track, he managed to get into a mediocre senior high in Xuhui District. Still, college remained an impossible dream for him. Then education reform gave him the reprieve he needed, although on his first try he only got a measly 217 points in the entrance exam. The family was aghast; no one would give him a place at university, even if you paid them. But the following year he sat it again, and to everyone's relief, he was finally accepted by a third-rate university in Shanghai to study marketing, the most unpromising trade.

I went to college in Shanghai, graduating from East China Normal University in '98. The family wanted me to commute to school, but I insisted on living on campus. This had the effect of me, the good girl at home, rapidly degenerating into a punk rocker, charging all over the city to underground gigs, smoking and drinking, and generally cursing my head off. Anyone I liked was the dog's bollocks; others were twats. It was around '98 that the Internet really got going. I began to spend my time writing short stories in Internet cafés, buried myself in chat rooms, and had online friends from all over the world. Bidding goodbye to my age of innocence, I even had a tryst with an indie youth from Beijing. Whenever I went home, and saw my brother's gormless face, I couldn't help thinking that we were slowly drifting apart. I was fearless and free, but he was lost in twatsville.

My brother gained lot of weight in high school. With the patinated wire-framed glasses he wore to correct his near-sightedness, he looked quite stupid. All the other boys had some sort of hobby, even if it was just watching cartoons or playing football. My brother was the perfect example of someone without a life. He didn't like reading or sport; he didn't even watch a lot of television. As someone born in the '80s, he had no idea what New Concept Literature was, he didn't know the difference between Adidas and Nike, and he'd never been to People's Square on his own. I couldn't see what pleasure he got from life at all, until one night, somewhere near the new apartment buildings, I saw someone collapsed on the ground, surrounded by a group of teenagers shouting, "Milk Tea! Milk Tea!" That was Shuangfeng's nickname, but I didn't believe it could be him. I went over, and it was him, passed out from drinking. I tried to lift him but he was too heavy so I ended up getting four of his mates to help carry him home. On the way back I berated them for drinking at their age. "Don't look at us," said one, "your brother was the one who downed eighteen pints." I was shocked. One of the girls who had come along pulled at my sleeve, "You won't be too hard on him, will you? He's under a lot of stress."

What stress? No one even told him off when he came to the next day, because Grandpa, the tolerant and understanding educator, rejected that approach, in spite of or exactly because of the seriousness of the matter. After a long heart-to-heart with the family, Shuangfeng swore he would never drink again. A few days later, he was carried home again drunk as mud. After watching the same scene repeated so many times, I realized that drinking was what my brother did for a hobby. I couldn't really believe it: a boy of eighteen, a drunkard? Surely that sort of thing only happened in novels, and yet it really did happen to my own little brother.

After university I got a job at a fashion magazine. My punk days were over. I got myself some designer clothes and handbags, changed my image, and became fashionable and fashion conscious. That same year my brother started university, but because I had set such a bad example Mum and Dad wouldn't allow him to live on campus. So life for him was no different than when he was at high school. He ate rice porridge in the morning, went off to college, and then biked home in the afternoon. One day he asked for my advice: how to escape from his own personal house arrest. I thought for a moment, and said, "How about joining a club, at least you'll be able to stay out a little longer." A couple of days later, he told me he'd been accepted by the college football team. Yet again, this confounded my expectations. He was fat, wore glasses and had calluses and flat feet. I just couldn't imagine him sprinting around a field. I later learned that he'd given his new Samsung Anycall, worth about two thousand yuan, to the team captain, and bought himself a cheap second-hand Motorola with his pocket money. He'd also told the captain, "My sister's interviewed such and such celebrity, maybe she could get you an autograph." The captain was really into that particular celebrity, almost as much as he liked Samsung mobiles, and that was how he got himself accepted.

At last, I saw in my brother some talent for social life. I went to see him play a few times: running around the lousy pitch were a crew of total misfits mucking about with a football. Shuangfeng was wearing the No. 7 Man United shirt and Nike football boots I'd given him. His Levis were draped over the crossbar of his Giant ten-speed mountain bike. His Jeansport rucksack hung off the handlebars. He really stood out. A group of girls were always hanging about watching the game. "No. 7 looks pretty cool," said one of them.

"Here's your chance for payback, Shuangfeng," I thought to myself. "I hope revenge is sweet."

Shuangfeng was at his peak then: he slimmed down and got all fit and muscly. His slanted eyes became less obvious with the white designer glasses I gave him, and even his goofy lips didn't seem to be a problem. "People reckon I look like Milan Baros," he told me. "Who's that?" I asked. "Center forward for the Czech national team. Plays for Liverpool," he said.

By that time, I was living with my boyfriend and wasn't at home very much. Mum told me that Shuangfeng was training like crazy. He could do more than a hundred press-ups and went running every morning. Though his flat feet meant he wasn't very fast, his stamina was amazing. He could run for an hour at a stretch. He even seemed to have found a girlfriend. More importantly, he still got drunk every once in a while, but no one could do anything about it now.

Then one evening having dinner at my parents, I heard a woman crying outside by the flowerbed and a man's voice shouting at her, "Shut your face! I'll kill you if you don't stop that noise." "Please, let me go! I'm begging you!" cried the woman. I went onto the balcony to have a look. It was completely dark and I couldn't make anything out. Then, loud and clear, I heard a slap. A woman screamed and burst into tears. Fearing the worst and worrying that the police wouldn't get here in time, I called down, "You violent bastard! The police are on their way." Unfortunately the man had no fear of the police. "I'll come up there and kill you! Believe it or not." He called back. Mum came over at that point and dragged me away saying, "What do you think you're doing? It's just the new tenant, an out-of-towner beating up his wife. He's drunk. He hits her every week." Then I heard the sound of someone running up the stairs. The bastard was actually coming to get us. Someone kicked at the door. At this point I got scared.

My brother walked out of his room. He had just done fifty press-ups and still had fifty to go. Bare-chested, he pulled the front door open and hit the lowlife in the face. He screamed and fell from our door to the end of the stairway. Shuangfeng stretched his neck this way and that in a very cool manner and then turned to me, "Just a drunken bastard," he said.

This was the first time in my entire life that I had seen my brother hit someone. Images of him been beaten up and blamed for things he didn't do, time and time again over the last twenty years went through my mind. "Little brother, you can stand on your own two feet at last," I thought, a trifle naively. At the same time I knew, you can't protect yourself from miseries and indignities life throws at you, even armed with a pair of sturdy fists.

My brother finally went public with his girlfriend.

She was a girl from Sichuan, in the year above him, called Lu Qinqin—acknowledged as one of the prettiest girls in college. I was pleased that Shuangfeng had found someone good-looking, but then he told me, "She doesn't have a very good reputation. She's had too many boyfriends." Then he added, "And she comes from a poor family." "You don't need to worry about that. You're only going out on a few dates," I said. Then I asked him how he managed to get her to go out with him. "She used to watch us play," he said. "Everyone knew her. Then one day my mates from the team dared me to try and pick her up," he said. "I stood at the college gates waiting for her. When she came out, I bought an ice pop, walked over, and said, 'Hey, woman, want one of these?' 'Get you!' she said. 'I reckon that guys should be as straightforward as I am,' I said. Then she agreed to come out with me."

"When you were at high school, there was that girl with the big eyes who was really into you," I said. "I chucked her." My blood ran cold remembering what he had said when he was small. Evidently he had been getting his own back for quite a while.

In 2004, before house prices in Shanghai shot up, Mum and Dad bought a new apartment and rented out the old one. When we moved into our new upmarket apartment, my brother brought Lu Qinqin over. She was rather quiet and very polite, a thin, pale girl, who I wouldn't say was exactly pretty. I don't know why, but she made me feel uneasy. She seemed burdened by a weight of sadness which sat oddly on her youthful shoulders. Sichuan girls are often mature for their age and tend to be pretty astute, capable and hardworking. My brother was obviously no match for her. After only a couple of sentences I could see that she had him under her thumb. Mum, of course, could see it too, and as a possible future Shanghai mother-in-law, she was not likely to stand for it. She turned to me and said, "She's not right for Shuangfeng."

That year my dad had been promoted to be the head of a medium-sized state enterprise and was flushed with his success. That evening after a few drinks at dinner Dad asked Lu Qinqin, "Hey, Little Lu! What do you think of our apartment? Decor's not bad, is it?" It was obvious that he had had a bit too much to drink and was showing off. "It's very nice, Mr. Wu," said Lu Qinqin. "I will bring my mum and dad to Shanghai one day and live in an apartment like this." "Shuangfeng has a lot of faults.

Mostly he drinks too much," said my dad. "You'll have to keep an eye on him." By this time Mum was glaring at him. It was obvious why. My parents hadn't officially acknowledged their relationship, but here was Dad talking as if they were already engaged. "Shuangfeng's a good person," she said, "but he is sometimes too naive, like a big kid." My mum rolled her eyes. I felt put out as well. Mum and I had always been very protective of Shuangfeng, and then along came another woman who felt just the same towards him. Of course we were going to resent her.

Lu Qinqin came to our house often since then. Sometimes I was there, sometimes I wasn't. I didn't really know the specifics, but then one day my brother rushed over in a state of distress. "Mum and Dad don't want me to see Lu Qinqin anymore!" I asked why. "They think her family is too poor," he said, "and she's an out-of-towner, so she must be after our money." "So, we've got two apartments, big deal!" I scoffed. "That's peanuts compared to the true rich." "That's just what Mum and Dad said!" said my brother.

"What if Lu Qinqin is only after your money?" I asked him seriously. "No way," he said. "I am not rich, there are richer people out there." "Very few people marry for love alone," I said. "Maybe the person she truly loves is completely penniless, and then there's this mega-rich guy chasing her but she doesn't like him at all, and so maybe you're her compromise in love and money." "You're only suspicious because she's not from round here."

What could I say? My brother was just twenty-two, only in his second year of university. At that age I was still making a nuisance of myself at gigs and staying up all night writing incomprehensible articles. He had always been quite immature for his age and had very little experience of the world. How could I expect him to understand something so complicated all at once.

Going out with someone is an expensive business. My brother had always been free with his money. Ever since he went to college I helped him out as well, so it is fair to say that he had no sense of economy at all. One month he blew more than a thousand yuan so Mum and Dad had to limit his spending money. They also wanted to remind him they could still tell him what to do. Then one day when he and Lu Qinqin had spent everything they had, she sighed. "We're so poor!" she said. My brother was desolate. Going home by himself through People's Square he saw a blood donation truck. "Right now I'd do anything," he thought. He pushed inside and told the doctor to take two hundred millilitres. But when he asked for money afterwards the doctor looked at him as if he was out of his mind and pointed to the slogan pasted on the truck. Bloody hell—"The gift of blood is a gift of life."

He went back to school with a carton of milk and told Lu Qinqin. "This is what I got for giving blood," he said. "I thought they would give me money but it turned out to be a donation truck." "Nowadays no one gives you money for giving blood anymore," Lu Qinqin told him. Then she said, "Shuangfeng, I will love you forever."

The funny thing was, two weeks later the school organized a "Give Blood" campaign. Because he didn't bother to explain himself, another two hundred millilitres of blood was taken from him. He nearly went cross-eyed. Luckily, as a healthy young man he pulled through and didn't pass out at the scene.

Lu Qinqin got a job as a personal assistant with the grand wage of one thousand five hundred yuan per month. You'll find girls like her all over Shanghai. My brother was in the year below her and had already started looking for job opportunities. Forget about the teaching of marketing techniques, most people who did marketing were worldly-wise and you couldn't possibly expect someone like Shuangfeng to do it on his own. My mum's idea was to get him into my dad's work-unit and that would be the end of it, but Dad had his reservations. For one, being the one in charge, he didn't think it was a good idea to have his son work under him; also, as he was about to retire in a few years time, once he left, they'd soon forget about him and where would that leave Shuangfeng? "Let Shuangfeng find his own way. There's nothing wrong with a few rejections." It was more like a wholesale free fall into nothing.

What I had worried about the most was about to happen. Shuangfeng had to get out there with his curriculum vitae and look for a job. There was no going back now. Whatever he went through at school, whether he had been bullied or the subject of praise, was irrelevant; the world out there probably couldn't even be bothered to pick on him before kicking him out the door. My boyfriend was the marketing manager for a foreign invested company so I asked him to come over and give my brother some interview tips. The two of them talked for an hour. Afterwards my boyfriend told me privately, "Your little brother doesn't even know the 4Ps of marketing. He can't even use PowerPoint. Who would ever give him a job? What did that shit college teach him anyway?" I sighed. "That shit college cost ten thousand a term."

At the beginning, things were more manageable, we just needed to find him an internship. I got him a placement at a company where a friend of mine worked. There was no pay, but he got a box meal at lunchtime. He had a computer, but my brother had no interest in computers whatsoever, so after a while, sitting there became like sitting on a bent pin. It just so happened that my friend was not the reliable kind either. Since she had known Shuangfeng for years, she ordered him around as if he were her little brother. Instead of giving him office work, she sent him off to get snacks from the shop downstairs. Soon the women employees of this loose organization, a crazy bunch, all sent him out on errands, buying chewing gum or soft drinks or cigarettes. By the end they'd even got him to go and buy sanitary towels for them. If he got the wrong ones they'd send him back to exchange them. In the two months he was there he didn't learn anything useful, but by the end of it he knew everything there was to know about sanitary towels: Unicharm, Carefree, everyday use, night use, with wings, ultra-thin, which girl used which kind, which brand was having a promotion, who usually had long periods and who had short ones. One day over dinner he told us all about it. My dad was livid. He gave me a piece of his mind and ordered Shuangfeng to hand in his notice.

My brother had no problem with buying sanitary towels—
he wasn't the least embarrassed about it—he was just a bit bored
of being around all those women, so he stopped going. My friend
called me, "Shuangfeng can't just pick and choose, you know. If
he carries on like this how will he ever get on?" "Just think about
it," I said, "if he'd stayed on at your place he'd have been selling
sanitary towels wholesale by now." "To be honest, the others only
asked him to go on errands for my sake," she said, "and of course
he's so cute and harmless. Most interns wouldn't get such an easy
time."

After that my brother tried out at all sorts of companies and
went with the same routine: interview, internship and be back
home after a couple of months. I helped him get through the
door of the first few companies, but after a while I got annoyed
with him too. I didn't want to fix things up for him anymore.
It was time for him to fend for himself for a change. He soon
realized that being sent out for sanitary towels hadn't been so
bad after all. The family hadn't expected much of him in the first
place and that year they rapidly lost all hope.

"What do you really want to do?" I asked him one day. He
thought for a bit, "I don't want to be stuck in an office. I hate
sitting in front of a computer, I'd prefer to have the chance to
walk about." I was flabbergasted. Note: Shanghai is full of recent
graduates trying to get into one of those state-of-the-art office
buildings. Getting a desk and a computer is like finding gold at
the end of a rainbow. "It sounds like you should be an express
courier or something," was all I could think to say.

I had always thought Shuangfeng was someone mediocre;
and it follows that his ideals and his behavior should also be
nothing out of the ordinary. I had no idea he actually had a
maverick streak in him.

"I want to go to police college and become a police officer,"
he said. "Isn't it hard to get into policing?" I said. "Don't you have
to have connections?" "It's not so bad in Shanghai. Our football
team captain got into police college completely on his own merit."

he replied. I encouraged him to have a go. To be honest I didn't take him seriously. Nothing seemed to go right for Shuangfeng. He only had to voice an idea for it to fall through. It was as if he suffered from some sort of curse.

Compared to my brother, Lu Qinqin was extremely driven. When she graduated she asked to live in our old apartment, but Mum and Dad refused. Their biggest concern was that it would affect the rental income, but it also reflected the fact that Mum and Dad had no intention of acknowledging her. This determined young woman from Sichuan was having such a hard time of it, renting a room with friends with a shared toilet and kitchen, but she did well at work and soon got a pay rise. That girl had vision. She had joined a yoga class whilst still at college. As yoga became popular in the city, she took a second job as a yoga instructor. Her monthly income from the two jobs now came to about eight thousand yuan, enough for a two bedroom flat in an old apartment building. She started wearing H&M or I.T. when she came to ours for dinner. And when I gave her a set of Yves Saint Laurent make-up, she obviously recognized the brand and thanked me several times.

Mum still hadn't warmed to her. In private she said to me, "Such expensive make-up. Why give it to Qinqin? Spoiling her will only make her spend more of Shuangfeng's money." I laughed and said, "You underestimate that girl. She's far more capable than Shuangfeng. In a few years she'll be standing on her own two feet." My mum sighed, "Once that happens she won't look at your brother anymore." "You say that because you know your son isn't up to much," I said. "I don't know what you have against her." "Well, she's from a poor family and she has no roots here, nothing to fall back on. However much she earns it doesn't mean a thing. As soon as a man with cash comes along, she'll be off like a shot. I think she's ambitious; there's no way your brother can support someone like that." "You may be right," I said. "Let's wait and see."

Life improved no end for my brother when Lu Qinqin got

her own flat. He stopped going to work, got drunk, and slept all day round at hers. We all thought he was working at some company as an intern. When Dad asked him after his graduation if he had been accepted as a formal employee, he finally let out the truth, "I stopped working ages ago. I stay at Lu Qinqin's place during the day." My dad nearly had a heart attack. He blamed Lu Qinqin for leading his son astray. "Dad, surely you should blame your son for his own failure," I said. "Look, if he works his butt off, she would be blamed for pressuring him; if he is lying about doing nothing, she would be blamed for allowing him to be an idler. How could any girl be so 'terrible'?" I had just got myself a new boyfriend, an out-of-towner who had come here to work. My mum, who had had enough, interrupted, "What is it with you two and these out-of-towners?" "What's so great about being from Shanghai anyway?" I said. "When the locals die, they'll have to be buried out of town anyway."

"Why can't you all just leave me alone!?" shouted Shuangfeng.

I flew into a rage and wagged my finger at him. "You sit there drinking all day long. Haven't you even noticed? You've turned into a complete fathead. You come from a good background. Kids a lot poorer than you are out there slogging their guts out and here you are, wasting your time doing press-ups, happy to live off your parents for the rest of your life. Loser!"

"I've lived in the shadow of this family all my life!" cried Shuangfeng.

Before I could lay into him, Dad jumped up, grabbed hold of a chair, and threw it at him, howling with rage. Shuangfeng bobbed and weaved to dodge the fists that coming his way. Dad had been a soldier in Tibet when he was young and even at fifty he could still pack a punch, but this was really the first time he had ever hit Shuangfeng. Seeing my fifty-year-old dad resorting to his fists to teach Shuangfeng a lesson, I began to cry.

The next day Shuangfeng turned up for an interview with a swollen face. He was shown the door as soon as he opened his mouth.

To be honest, I was well aware that the employment situation had been dire since 2004. Plenty of decent university graduates were unable to find a proper job. If even computer geeks and people educated abroad had to fight for a job, what chance would my brother have? If they were lucky, they might have apartments to rent out, bringing in an income more or less equal to an office worker's salary, this was the so-called locals' advantage. Some people might work their whole lives to get what Shuangfeng already had when he started out. But did that even count for anything anymore? They were just apartments. The streets were full of fiercely ambitious young people focusing their energy on getting ahead. Do you really think that in twenty years' time my brother would still be able to boast that he had two apartments?

Lu Qinqin's parents were coming to Shanghai. She had to work the day they arrived, so Shuangfeng asked me to drive him to the station to pick them up. He wanted to make a good impression. Chatting over dinner we learned that they were laid-off workers from Sichuan in considerable financial difficulties. In order to send their daughter to university, they had used up all their savings and were in deep debt. The old couple had ran a snack stall in the city centre but about a month ago it had been flattened by the city inspector, so they had no choice but to come to Shanghai and to stay with their daughter.

Mr. Lu was a middle-aged man of few words. He hardly said a thing, just sat there drinking white spirit shots with my brother. Lu Qinqin's mother liked to talk. She kept smiling at my brother as she chatted. She obviously really liked him. "Do you like Sichuan food, Little Wu?" she said. My brother nodded. "Well then, from now on your Auntie Lu will cook for you. You're welcome to come over whenever you like. Don't worry. Your Auntie Lu isn't going to sit at home doing nothing. I'm going to look for a supermarket job straight away." "Mrs. Lu, please don't talk like that." I said quickly. "This is Lu Qinqin's home. It has nothing to do with Shuangfeng. He has no right to ask anything of you." "But I like Shuangfeng," she said, "he's a good, kind boy.

I wasn't quite sure before I met him." My brother and I forced a smile.

Lu Qinqin's parents' arrival in Shanghai coincided with Dad going abroad on business so they weren't able to meet. My brother kept plotting this dinner, but Mum was continually on the alert to prevent it, because eating together would mean acknowledging the relationship between the two families. My brother had no choice but to trick Granny and Grandpa into meeting them. Grandpa was eighty. Older people don't tend to suspect ulterior motives so getting them to go along was easy. Shuangfeng seized the opportunity, and announced that he intended to marry Lu Qinqin. This put Grandpa in a rather awkward position. "But, you're only twenty-three," he said. "In the old days people got married at eighteen," Shuangfeng said. Grandpa rolled his eyes. "In the old days your parents decided whom you should marry and it was arranged through a matchmaker. I think you should go home and discuss it with your mum and dad." Yet again, things didn't go as my brother had planned. "You want to take a wife but you don't even have a job, Shuangfeng. That sort of thing would be out of the question even in the countryside, you know," said Granny mournfully.

My brother started taking stuff from home over to Lu Qinqin's apartment. At first it was just a spring bed that we didn't use, and extra quilts and pillows, but then he took our cooking oil, salt, soy sauce, and vinegar. He even gave his bike to Mr. Lu, telling us the story that it had been stolen. One day my mum was making dinner and couldn't find the cleaver. When she asked, it turned out Shuangfeng had taken that as well. "If I had that cleaver here I'd chop you up this instant!" spat my mother.

I saw how things were panning out. It was in the bag; Shuangfeng would soon be married. He was the sort of person who would present you with a fait accompli.

He appeared a few days later, completely mortified. "Lu Qinqin is seeing someone else," he said. I was surprised, though not that surprised—for his sake I acted astonished and asked him what had happened.

Lu Qinqin had been very secretive about it, he said. He hadn't noticed anything at first. I must admit, given his emotional IQ, it was highly unlikely my brother would have noticed that something was going on. Lu Qinqin's mum was the one who had told him. It seemed that she genuinely liked Shuangfeng and had let him know that lately there had been a man taking Lu Qinqin home after her yoga class. Maybe she had got to know him there. Distraught, Shuangfeng had rushed over to the yoga studio and laid in wait near the main door. Sure enough, he saw Lu Qinqin coming out with a man.

With the stuffing knocked out of him, my brother couldn't summon the courage to confront them. Instead he biked home, told me what had happened, and then tore open the special edition Maotai that Dad had been saving for ten years and drank the whole lot. Still not drunk, he found the cooking wine, drank half the bottle, collapsed on the sofa, and fell asleep.

It was late. My mum had gone to bed much earlier and had no idea what was happening. I stood there for a while looking at his drunken form and thinking to myself: "When he wakes up he's going to wreck the house." I decided to go and see Lu Qinqin. Her mother opened the door. She guessed why I'd come as it was so late, and let me in, apologetically. Lu Qinqin was on the phone. I looked around the room and saw all the stuff from our house: our spring bed, our quilt, our calendar, our alarm clock, our slippers, and our kitchen cleaver. Lu Qinqin ended the phone call, let her mother go back to bed, and made me a cup of tea. Then we discussed my brother.

"That guy, he's just a friend," said Lu Qinqin. "Don't get me wrong. I didn't come over to accuse you," I said. The man was a colleague from work, she explained, the manager of the marketing department. He did Taekwondo at the gym and when he noticed Lu Qinqin teaching yoga, he was intrigued and came over to chat. She didn't want the company to know she had another job, so she had no choice but to go for a coffee with him a couple of times. When he asked to take her home, she found it difficult to refuse. Little by little they got to know one another. He could be interested in her; it just wasn't out in the open yet. "I don't think I've behaved very well," she said, finally.

"You can't say that," I said, "this sort of thing could happen to anyone. I just hope that one day, if you give up on my brother, you don't hurt him too badly." "I like Shuangfeng so much," she said, "but he's just a big kid. I can't rely on him for anything." "He's tried very hard to prove he can contribute," I sighed, looking at all the things he had taken from our house. Lu Qinqin shook her head and said, "This isn't what I want. I'm under such a lot of pressure. It's me who has to repay all the money my family owes. I hope that he has a future of his own and will not ask for his family for help. Is it wrong for a girl to hope her man to have a future and do well?"

She kept shaking her head. "I have never been able to rely on him," she said. "Maybe he should find a girl from Shanghai, someone well-off, and then he'd have no worries for the rest of his life. He has always been such a child. But strangely enough, that's what I love about him," she said. "I don't know what to do. I'm so confused."

"So ... well ... what have you decided?" I asked her.

"Shuangfeng said he wanted to try for police college," she said. "I think I should wait until after his exam to decide."

So that's what held their relationship together. Lu Qinqin said she didn't want anything to affect him emotionally before his exams but she also wanted to wait and see whether my brother was capable of turning himself around. After all, a police officer is similar in status to a civil servant. Being a policeman would be a brilliant future for someone like my brother. But with his lack of EQ, I had a hard time believing that he would be capable of catching any bad guys; I'd just be thankful if he didn't harm any good guys.

"I'm definitely going to get into the police college!" announced my brother.

He had made similar boasts before his high school exams, before his university entrance exams, and before his CET-4 (College English Test band 4), but the results hadn't been anything to write home about. My mum and dad were really happy about it though, thinking that this time, their son was going to do them proud. My dad announced, "If you get in I'll drink my special edition Maotai that I have treasured for ten years!" He opened the cabinet, "Eh? Where is my Maotai?"

That year the police college was taking on two hundred new recruits, more than ever before, but only this year's university graduates could apply. That meant if my brother didn't get in this time, he wouldn't get another opportunity. The exam was made up of a written exam, a physical ability test, and an interview. All he had to do was train hard, and work hard at his studies. He shaved his head and he started wearing contact lenses. He got all muscly again, the few times we went out together with my mates they took quite a shine to him.

But he flunked it.

Apparently he had only concentrated on anaerobic exercise. Sure, you need muscle strength to do press-ups and pull-ups, but the police college's exam was about physical stamina: a five-thousand-meter run. My brother knew this, but oddly he had neglected the running exercises, doing strength training instead. Another proof that he had the maverick streak.

His rainbow-colored world turned monochrome. I hadn't had high expectations for him, but still I had hoped for the best. Now I was certain that even this monochrome world would soon collapse. Lu Qinqin and Shuangfeng wouldn't last much longer.

This time, it was Shuangfeng who hurt Lu Qinqin's feeling. One day, during a quarrel about nothing, my brother roared, "Why don't you just go off with that marketing manager of yours!" Lu Qinqin slapped him right there in the middle of the street, jumped into a taxi, and disappeared.

Shuangfeng had a group of slacker mates from his football days; simple-minded meatheads, the lot of them. They had a really stupid idea: text her, and say you have a new girlfriend. If she begs you to come back, that means she loves you. If she doesn't, it means she's gone off with the marketing manager. My brother, not having a clue about girls, did as he was told. She texted back later that day: "Let's split up then."

The day they broke up Lu Qinqin asked Shuangfeng to introduce her to his new girlfriend. My brother didn't know how to get out of it, so he asked me to come along. The break-up took place in a tiny park in city center. It was deserted. Cars and trucks whizzed by on the overpass, and the tree leaves were covered in dust. Standing next to Lu Qinqin was a tall man in a track suit. He looked pretty ordinary but you could tell that he thought he was some kind of Johnny Depp. I asked my brother in private whether this was the marketing manager. He scratched his head, "I've forgotten what he looked like."

Of course it was him.

"Why haven't you brought your new girlfriend, Wu Shuangfeng?" asked Lu Qinqin. "I haven't got a new girlfriend," replied my brother. "I was trying to trick you." I couldn't believe it. How could he be so silly? Was this really the time to admit such a thing? As I expected, Lu Qinqin gave him a despairing look. "Why are we here then?" she said. "To get things straight that you're the one who was seeing someone else," said my brother. "Shuangfeng, you're beginning to get on my nerves now," she said.

"So this is your new boyfriend," my brother counter-attacked. "Not up to much, is he?" The new boyfriend turned to look at the cars on the overpass and smiled. "Let's not hurt each other, Wu Shuangfeng," said Lu Qinqin. "From now on, let's pretend we never met." "Okay," said my brother.

And so just like that he let her go. She and the boyfriend were already at the exit when Shuangfeng suddenly called out, "Hey you! Do you want a fight?" Johnny Depp turned, looked at Lu Qinqin, then looked at me. "That's not cool, man, there are ladies here," he said slowly. I dismissed him with my hand, "Don't mind me. Come and have a go if you think you're hard enough." "I've no intention of fighting, it will cause pain," said the boyfriend. "Anyway, I thought you wanted to be a policeman? You won't have much chance if you get arrested for fighting." "I didn't pass," said my brother. Once again, this was too much information. It was an idiotic thing to say.

"Come on kid, fighting never solves anything. You'll realize that soon enough," he said. "What's that got to do with anything?" I sneered. "You're just not up to it." The boyfriend looked at me, unriled. He took Lu Qinqin in his arms and walked off.

On the way home Shuangfeng said, "You were supposed to calm things down." "I was hoping he'd Taekwondo you to a pulp," I said savagely.

That night Shuangfeng suddenly broke down. The entire household crawled out of bed to comfort him. The old people tried everything but it was no use, so in the end they rang and told me to come over. My brother said he wanted to talk to me alone. There was no soul searching; to my surprise he said, "I'm so cut up, Sis. The week before we broke up I went to her place and we had sex six times." I couldn't believe it. "Six times?" I said. "She held me tight, and said she wanted to be with me until the end." I sighed, "And you still have no idea what she really feels about you?" "No," said my brother. After a while I couldn't help saying, "Bollocks! Six times in one day? Did you take anything?" "Why should I? I'm pretty fit," said my brother. "Bloody hell, you may die of it!" I exclaimed.

Lu Qinqin had lost her virginity to him, he said, and so he'd always thought she'd marry him, but it had all gone off-track, and he was hurting. "It doesn't matter," I consoled him. "It was your first time too, so you don't owe each other anything." "That wasn't my first time. I lost my virginity to that girl with the big eyes at high school." I nearly fainted with annoyance. "When was that?" I asked. "In the summer holidays after the first school year," he said. I did a quick calculation. I would have been in the second year of university. I had sex for the first time that year, and I'm five years older. The more I thought about it the more furious I got. "You were too young to do that sort of thing, you little bugger! You deserve everything you get! Stupid idiot, cry your heart out!" I fumed.

After his split with Lu Qinqin, my brother's football mates talked him into running a milk tea shop. None of them had any luck with proper jobs and they were just hanging out and doing nothing all day. One of them knew someone who ran a milk tea franchise, and he wanted to get out and look for business opportunities somewhere else. And they decided to take over his business.

My brother talked to the family: my dad decided the boy would be irredeemably lost if he carried on as he was, so he agreed to plough in his hard-earned savings and make my brother the main shareholder. He invested eighty thousand yuan, and Shuangfeng took on a shop-front not quite a meter wide. The previous owner had left, and it was only when my brother and his mates were stocking up that they realized he still owed the head office tens of thousands of yuan in payment for goods. It was up to my brother to pay this back. My mum and dad were spitting blood again. He hadn't even started and the shop was already losing money.

"Milk Tea" was my brother's nickname, so now Milk Tea sold milk tea, and everyone thought that was great. I went over to have a look. The little shop was bright and bustling. It was opposite a bus stop so foot traffic wasn't an issue. The milk tea my brother made tasted better than anything you could buy on the street. Watching him working skillfully behind the counter, taking payment and giving change, I felt a sliver of comfort at last. "Oh Shuangfeng, if only this could be the start of something good!" I said to myself. Having a look around as I drove home I discovered that within a strip of about a kilometer, there were at least ten other milk tea shops. My heart once again dropped to the bottom of the sea.

There is no question that the shop was losing money. It lost about five thousand yuan every month. He worked very hard. He delivered tea in the pouring rain, falling off his bike and breaking it in the process. He manned the shop from nine in the morning until ten at night, and never compromised on the quality of ingredients, but in this competitive world it just wasn't enough, even for a small taste of success. Maybe that's just how it is on the street. Success has nothing to do with whether you work hard or not. Around that time, the stock market was booming. My mum would like to profit more from the market by investing more, but she had to give my brother five thousand a month. She'd had no choice.

One day my brother was alone in the shop. Light from the sunset lit up the street, and Lu Qinqin appeared before him. "A milk tea please. No pearls," she said. Then she recognized him. "You're running a milk tea shop now, Wu Shuangfeng?" she asked. My brother nodded. He noticed she was wearing a purple anti-radiation dress.

"I'm pregnant," said Lu Qinqin.

"Did you marry the marketing manager?" my brother asked.

"No, I married someone from Hong Kong," she said. "I live nearby. I had no idea you were here."

That day my brother took her home on the back of his bike. She didn't live very far away. She could come over for milk tea often. When they were saying goodbye she said, "Shuangfeng, I came to know you during the worst part of your life. It's just my bad luck." My brother didn't speak. Hurt, she said, "You were the worst boyfriend I ever had but, remember this; I was the best girl you'll ever know." Confused, and sad, my brother watched as she walked slowly into her building. He rode back to the shop and thought for a while. Then he turned off the power, rolled down the metal door, and declared the tea shop bankrupt.

He never saw Lu Qinqin again.

My parents pulled some strings, and got my brother a logistics job in a loft complex. Compared to a lot of jobs, it wasn't so bad. He didn't have to sit in front of a computer, he just had to put up with the boss's ugly face. There were a few girls after him, all from Shanghai. I said to him that it might be time for him to have a proper girlfriend, he was already twenty-four. "I want to wait until I get into police college," he said. I was surprised. He still had a chance at being a policeman? The World Expo was just around the corner, he told me. This time they weren't only recruiting that year's graduates, but last year's as well. There were a relatively large number of places. This was his last opportunity. At the dinner table, Granny said, mournfully, "Close your mouth this time, Shuangfeng. You were rejected last time, you know, because you didn't close your mouth."

This time Shuangfeng prepared well for the exam. He gave up drinking, studied every day, did running and strength training, and even had an operation to fix his eyesight once and for all. No one in the family held out any hope, they just let him get on with it, but I could tell that my brother's lousy luck was about to run its course.

He passed the physical exam, the written exam, and the interview easily. Last of all came the running, the same five-thousand-meter run.

When I went with him to the playing field where the test was held that day, he was nervous. "There's something I'd like to tell you," I began. "I've just split up with my boyfriend." "If you go on like this you'll end up on the shelf," he replied, "you're nearly thirty." "Look, if a talented girl like me still can't find a husband, but there are still girls after you even after you've messed up so badly, then nothing's fair." "Bollocks," said my brother, "it's just that Shanghai boys are popular for some reason."

He started to get ready and took out a pair of faded trainers. "What happened to the brand-named trainers I gave you?" I asked. "Lu Qinqin gave me these. I haven't worn them since we split up, and I will never wear them again after today," he replied. "Do your best," I said. "If you fail, there won't be another chance, unless you want to be a city inspector." "That won't happen. I'm going to win it for you. Just you wait and see."

As he walked to the starting line, he turned, "I really am going to win it for you."

It started drizzling. My brother was at the centre of the pack of twenty. He moved in and out of sight among the runners. The leader was a skinny boy, the perfect build for running, much better proportioned and lighter on his feet than my brother. Next to me was a middle-aged couple, who I guessed were his parents. They spoke with a rural Nanhui District accent. "Our Jianguo is going to win it this time!" they sounded very excited.

You didn't have to win the race, if you were among the first five in your group you were basically safe. But it was police college and everyone wanted to win.

The boy from Nanhui ran like a deer in the fine rain, gradually leaving the rest behind. He looked great as he ran, even giving his parents a wave as he passed us. His serious face wet with rain, Shuangfeng didn't glance my way at all.

About half-way through I noticed Shuangfeng was five meters behind the boy from Nanhui. The rest were trailing about half a circuit behind. He flashed past me, and I couldn't help but call out, "Shuangfeng! Go for it!" The rain got heavier. "Win it for me, Shuangfeng!" I called after him.

I remembered him being chased and beaten by the other boys when he was small. I recalled the pain and the hurt. "So you think you can outrun it all, Shuangfeng." I watched him pounding intently towards the finish line. I imagined him standing before me in police uniform. If only it had happened a year earlier. My dear brother, the world is just that simple, so long as you run fast enough, right?

In the final dash he was right behind the Nanhui boy. A second from the finish line where we were all waiting, the boy from Nanhui shouted, "Hey Ma, I'm in!" to the middle-aged couple beside me, and in that second, my brother passed him.

I couldn't see clearly the look on my brother's face.

Stories by Contemporary Writers from Shanghai